Blue Ribbon
Trail Ride

Horses and Friends Series

A Horse for Kate
Silver Spurs
Mystery Rider
Blue Ribbon Trail Ride

MIRALEE FERRELL

Blue Ribbon Trail Ride

DAVID C COOK
transforming lives together

BLUE RIBBON TRAIL RIDE
Published by David C Cook
4050 Lee Vance Drive
Colorado Springs, CO 80918 U.S.A.

Integrity Music Limited, a Division of David C Cook
Eastbourne, East Sussex BN23 6NT, England

The graphic circle C logo is a registered trademark of David C Cook.

LCCN 2015933709
ISBN 978-1-4347-0736-9
eISBN 978-0-7814-1426-5

© 2016 Miralee Ferrell
Published in association with Tamela Hancock Murray of The Steve
Laube Agency, 5025 N. Central Ave., #635, Phoenix, AZ 85012

The Team: Don Pape, Ingrid Beck, Ramona Cramer Tucker, Nick
Lee, Amy Konyndyk, Tiffany Thomas, Susan Murdock
Cover Design: DogEared Design, Kirk DouPonce

Printed in the United States of America
First Edition 2016

5 6 7 8 9 10 11 12 13 14

073018

*To Kate, my darling granddaughter.
I hope by the time you're old enough
to read these books, you'll love horses
and reading as much as I do.*

Chapter One

Thirteen-year-old Kate Ferris and her best friend, Tori Velasquez, lay on a pile of loose hay in the loft above the stalls in the barn Kate's family owned. Kate rolled onto her stomach and propped herself on her elbows. "I love working here, but I'm glad the chores are done this early in the day. It's so hot."

Tori batted at a fly that tried to land on her face. "Yuck. I hate flies. It sure would be nice to go swimming, but the Hood River pool is too far."

"I know. I already asked Mom, and she said we'll have to wait until she's going to town. What do you want to do now? I don't feel like riding in this heat, even if we don't often have the arena to ourselves. Want to turn on the sprinkler and get cooled off?"

Tori sat up and opened her mouth to speak, then shut it as Kate pointed below. Kate's parents walked across the arena and headed toward the office.

Kate peered over the edge of the loft. She lifted her hand and started to wave, but something about her mother's expression stopped her. Instead, she placed her finger to her lips and shook her head at Tori.

It wasn't that Kate wanted to spy on her parents, but something was up, and she wanted to know what. She scrambled to think of anything she might have done wrong, but nothing came to mind. She and her friends had been helping Mrs. Maynard, an older neighbor up the road, with her chores, and Kate had finished everything in the barn and house that Mom had asked, so that couldn't be what put a frown on her mother's face.

Mom paused outside the office door. "It makes me sick that we can't do it, John. That camp has such a great reputation for helping autistic kids, and it's amazing they still have openings. Isn't there any way we could swing it?"

"I'm sorry, Nan. I don't see how. This boarding stable is close to paying its way, but the first month, it cost more than it brought in."

Kate's heart jolted. Mom and Dad weren't thinking of shutting it down, were they? She stared at Tori, who looked nervous.

Her friend must be thinking the same thing. Kate leaned forward again, hoping that wasn't where this conversation was headed.

"I know. But I think we'll turn a profit this month. The horse show gave us excellent advertising."

"Which is great," Kate's dad said. "And as long as that continues, we'll keep it open. But we still don't have the extra it would take for Pete's camp. I'm sorry, honey. It's not in our budget this summer, unless God gives us a miracle."

Kate's mom nodded. "Let's take one more look at the books, but I know you're right, John. It breaks my heart Pete can't go, when it could be such a help in his progress."

Kate's dad opened the door to the office and let her mom go in first, then he followed and shut it behind him.

Kate sucked in a breath. "Wow. I thought for sure they were going to say they were closing the barn."

Tori made a face. "Me too. I'm thankful they aren't, but I'm thinking about Pete. That camp sounds awesome."

"This is the first I've heard of it. I'm surprised Mom and Dad didn't say anything before."

"Maybe they didn't want to get Pete's hopes up. He might not talk a lot, but he's a smart kid."

"I know." Kate thought for a moment. "How about we call Colt and Melissa and see if we can figure out a way to make enough money to send Pete to camp?"

Tori pushed to her knees, her brown eyes sparkling. "Cool! Let's go."

Kate followed Tori down the ladder to the lower level. "We'd better keep our voices down. Mom and Dad might think we were spying on them."

She felt bad that she'd wanted to listen, and even worse that the first thing she'd thought about was losing the boarding stable, while Tori's first comment had been about Pete. But right now she was glad she'd been in the barn loft, or they'd never have known her family couldn't afford the camp. Somehow she and her friends had to find a way to make it happen.

A short while later Kate and her three friends sat in the shade of the towering fir tree in the backyard after cooling off in the sprinkler. Kate lifted a glass of lemonade and took a long drink, then set it on the small table near her lawn chair. "I'm glad you guys could come over and help us plan."

Colt, their thirteen-year-old friend who homeschooled and rode Western, switched a piece of straw to the other side of his mouth. "I've heard about that camp for autistic kids. Mom has a friend who was a cabin leader one year, and she told us how awesome it is. The kids all seem to love it. It's a bummer it costs so much."

Melissa, who'd once been one of the most popular girls in school, settled into a chair on the other side of Colt. "Your little brother is such a sweet kid, Kate. He deserves to go."

Tori nodded. "I agree. That's why we wanted the two of you to come help us figure out a way to raise money."

Kate leaned forward. "I've been thinking. Wouldn't it be great if we could put together some type of horse-related event that the entire community could take part in? And we could make autism the focus of the fund-raiser. Pete would benefit, but if we raised enough money, other kids might be able to go to camp too."

"Cool!" Colt grinned so wide, he almost lost the straw from the corner of his lips, but he tucked it back in. "Anybody have any brilliant ideas of a horse event that would bring in serious money?"

Melissa flipped her blonde hair over her shoulder. "Well, if it's to benefit special kids like Pete, I'll bet a lot of the townspeople might get involved. What do you think about some kind of trail ride where people win prizes?"

Kate exhaled. "I love it. Way to go, Melissa." It never failed to surprise her how smart and kind Melissa had turned out to be, once she got over being stuck-up. A twinge of guilt hit Kate. That wasn't fair. Melissa hadn't been stuck-up as much as she'd been hurt in the past by friends who misjudged her and used her when they thought she was wealthy.

Sure, Melissa had been unkind to her and Tori in the beginning, but she later admitted a lot of it was because she was jealous of them. That had totally stunned Kate. The popular, pretty girl jealous of them! But Melissa had envied Kate's family life, and now Kate understood why. Melissa's mom had allowed her divorce and loss of their money to push her to drink and yell at Melissa a lot. Since Kate, Tori, and Colt had accepted Melissa and taken her into their circle of friends, the girl had changed into someone they enjoyed having around.

Tori frowned. "I don't get it. How can a trail ride bring in money and let people win prizes? The prizes would cost us money, right? And wouldn't they have to be awfully big to make anyone want to pay to take part?"

"Actually, it's a great idea." Colt rubbed his chin. "When I lived in Montana, I went on a trail ride like that, but it was a scavenger hunt. We had a great turnout, and horse clubs from all over took part. The sponsors hid items along the trail. Participants were given clues and had to hunt for the items. There was a big prize at the end for the person who found the most items, but there were a lot of prizes for people who came in second and third—even riders who found all the items but didn't get there fast. We could do age categories to make it fair."

Tori waved her hand. "I still don't get it. How would we pay for the prizes? From the entry fee people pay?"

Kate shook her head. "Nope. All of that money would go into the fund. We'd ask businesses in Hood River and here in Odell to donate gift certificates or items from their stores as prizes. Right, Colt?"

"Right. Some of the businesses in Montana donated really cool stuff. The barn that sponsored the ride took out ads in the paper. You know, the *Hood River News* would probably give us a free ad, since it's a fund-raiser."

Tori groaned. "So, let's see if I get this right. Who goes out and asks all these businesspeople and the newspaper to donate stuff?"

Melissa gave one of her old smirks. "We do, silly. But hey, it's not a big deal. I've done fund-raising with the Pony Club." She lowered her head. "When I used to belong, I mean."

Kate's heart lurched at the pain in Melissa's voice. She'd wondered if Melissa had dropped out of the club, since her family no longer had the money. "Great! Then you can be our expert and make sure we know what to say. You did an awesome job getting us organized for the parade we rode in during Fort Dalles Days."

"Seriously?" Melissa's voice squeaked. "You want me to be in charge again? Why?"

Kate smiled. "Because you're a natural leader, that's why."

"But I might mess it up. What if no one wants to give anything?" A note of panic crept into her words. "Some of the people in town knew my dad, and since he left …"

Tori reached out her hand and grabbed Melissa's. "That's not going to happen, Melissa. Like Kate said, you're good at this stuff, and we trust you. Nothing's going to go wrong. Just you wait and see."

Chapter Two

An hour later, Kate was so excited, she could barely stand still. Her parents had approved the idea of a trail-ride fund-raiser that would ultimately be a scavenger hunt on horseback. They'd been hesitant at first, but Melissa and Colt had done a great job explaining and convincing them it would work.

Kate's mom tapped her fingers on the kitchen countertop. "Are the four of you ready to go now, or do you want to wait until another day to get started?"

Kate's enthusiasm dimmed as it dawned on her what Mom was suggesting. "You think we should start asking for donations now? Yikes, Mom! I don't think we're ready to do that yet."

Tori edged closer to where Kate stood. "If your mom is willing to drop us off in downtown Hood River, we could hit a few places today. Or we could ride our bikes to the Odell grocery store and start there."

Colt nodded. "Great idea, Tori. It might be best to talk to a couple of businesses closer to home before we go to Hood River."

Melissa shook her head. "I don't agree. We're not ready. We don't have any flyers to hand out that tell about the camp or the trail ride. Who's going to believe four kids who come walking in asking for stuff, when we aren't even prepared?"

Kate grinned. "And this is exactly why we put Melissa in charge, so we don't do stupid stuff and look like idiots." She raised her hand for a high five.

Melissa slapped it and giggled. "Thanks. I thought you'd be mad that I was shooting down your mom's plan. How about we get on the computer and see what we can come up with? We can print a few handouts here. Then if it's okay with you, Mrs. Ferris, we could ride our bikes to the grocery store in Odell and practice on the owner."

Kate's mom pulled a mug from the cupboard. "If you get something finished, and you want me to look at it before you print it, I'll be happy to help. And if there's time, I'll run you down to the grocery store so you can talk to Mr. Jacobs."

"Cool!" Colt waved toward the doorway. "Kate, lead the way to the computer. I'm not very good at this stuff, but I'm guessing Melissa is—or Tori … or you."

Kate rolled her eyes. "So you're pretty much worthless, is that what you're saying? You aren't going to back out on talking to people, are you?"

"No way. I think I'd make a killer salesman." He shot her a cocky look and waggled his eyebrows.

Tori groaned. "Come on, let's get to work."

Thirty minutes later, Kate and her friends stared at the computer screen. "Awesome," Kate said. "That looks really professional. Good job, Melissa and Tori."

Melissa ducked her head. "Thanks. Let's show it to your mom before we print a copy." She shoved back her chair.

Kate's mom stood in the open doorway. "No need to get up." She walked to the desk and leaned over Melissa's shoulder. "Hmm. You have the name—Blue Ribbon Trail Ride. That's good. Do you want to say anything about the date or how much it will cost to take part in the ride?"

Tori shook her head. "We were thinking we should put that in the flyers we hang around town or send to other horse clubs or barns. Right now we figured we only need information a business would want to know. Right, guys?"

Melissa nodded. "Right. We could say that the donations will be used for prizes, if you think we should."

"It wouldn't hurt," Kate's mom said. "You don't want too much information, but you need all the details a business would expect to see. You might mention that we're hoping to raise enough to fund a scholarship for autistic campers, and we'll put on all our flyers the names of businesses that donate."

"Great." Melissa swiveled to the computer screen and started to type. When she finished, she looked up. "What do you think?"

"Perfect. Print it, then let's head to the store so you kids can try out Colt's super-salesmanship." Kate's mom ruffled his hair and chuckled. "I'll go tell Dad so he can come in and watch Pete."

"I guess I stuck my foot in my mouth big-time, huh?" Colt gave a sheepish smile. "One of the girls might be a better spokesperson than me."

Kate snorted. "No way! You said you'd make a killer salesman, and we're going to let you prove it."

It only took a couple of minutes to print half a dozen copies of the handout, then Kate and her friends followed her mom to their Subaru Outback.

"I'm so nervous." Kate buckled her seat belt and peered over her shoulder at her friends. "Colt, you should be sitting up here, since you're going to do the talking."

He pulled the piece of straw from his mouth. "Naw. I figure whoever sits in the front seat should be the first one to talk, since it makes you look more official. Besides, girls are *such* good talkers, there's no way you can fail."

He grunted as Tori and Melissa both poked him in the ribs with their elbows. "Hey, what did I say?"

Neither one replied, but as soon as the car rolled to a stop in the grocery-store parking lot, they pushed open their doors and got out. Tori looked at Kate as she shut the front door. "So, are you going to do the talking?"

Kate wiped the palms of her hands on her jeans. She didn't want to look like a wimp to her friends, but her stomach was in knots. This hadn't sounded hard when they'd talked about it at home, or when she thought Colt or even Melissa would do the talking. "What if I mess up? And what do I ask them to donate? Groceries? Melissa would do a better job than I would."

Mom leaned against the car hood. "You could suggest a gift certificate but also tell them it's up to them what they'd like to donate, if they do anything at all. Don't make it sound like you expect it, but let them know you appreciate anything they're willing to give. Oh—and always ask to speak to the owner or manager." She smiled. "I'm guessing it will help that Mr. Jacobs knows your dad. Be sure to tell him who you are."

Kate nodded. "Okay, I guess." She turned toward Colt. "But I still think Melissa or Colt is the best choice. He's always so laid back and sensible about everything, and Melissa's in charge."

He held up his hand. "Tell you what. While you're in there, Melissa can tell me how it's done, and I'll do the next one. Promise."

Melissa tipped her head to the side. "You need to do this one, Kate. Your family knows the owner, and I don't. Quit worrying. You'll do great."

Kate squared her shoulders and faced the entrance to the store, feeling as if she'd been sent to the principal's office. The worst Mr. Jacobs could do was say no and kick them out of the store for bugging him, right? And maybe one or two business owners would care about their cause and bless them by contributing prizes. There was no way she'd find out unless she tried. She wasn't sure how she'd gotten saddled with this responsibility, but maybe it was only right that she be the one to talk first, since it was her brother they were trying to help. The thought of Pete lifted her spirits, and she strode forward with more confidence than she'd ever thought she could muster.

Mom's voice halted her several yards from the car. "Kate? Want me to come too?"

Kate wanted that more than anything at the moment, but she shook her head. "Thanks. I'm good." This was her idea—hers and her friends'—and she'd do it with their help, or not at all.

Fifteen minutes later Kate and Tori came out of the store. Kate felt as though she'd won the biggest prize ever offered at any horse show. She waited until they were almost to the car, then twirled in a happy circle. "Awesome!"

Her mother's expression went from serious to excited in a second. "Good news, I take it?"

"Yeah!" Kate grabbed Tori and swung her around. "We nailed it!"

Melissa laughed and gave Kate a high five as she spun past. "You mean *you* nailed it. Colt, you're going to have to work your tail off to beat what Kate did."

Colt's eyes sparkled. "Yep. That's a fact. I say we let her be our spokesman from now on. Why take a chance of messing things up when we have Kate on our team?"

Kate sobered and stopped in front of him. "No way. You said you'd do it next."

"I know, but you just got an awesome pledge. I was hoping for maybe twenty-five."

"All I did was think about Pete and other kids like him, and it made me realize I was being silly to worry about what I'd say or what the owner would think. I forgot about me and kept thinking about how great it will be if we raise enough money so Pete and at least one or two other kids can go to that camp."

Kate's mom slipped her arm around Kate's shoulders and squeezed. "How wonderful, honey. I'm proud of you."

Tori grinned. "That's so cool—and you didn't act even a little bit scared when you were talking. I'm going to remember that next time I have to do something that freaks me out. I'll think about somebody else instead of myself, and maybe it'll help."

Kate smiled. "Trust me. It works." She turned to her mother. "We're on a roll. Do you care if we hit the other businesses in Odell while we're here, since it's all of a block long? It's not like we can get lost or anything."

"Sure. Go for it. I brought a book. But I have a suggestion that might make it go faster. Since Colt offered to go next, and you did so well, Kate, how about you split into two teams, and the two of you be the spokespeople next time. Then Melissa and Tori can do it if they want a turn."

Tori kicked at a rock on the pavement. "But what if we—or I—don't want to? Is that bad?"

"Not at all." Kate's mom patted Tori's arm. "Not everyone likes or is good at the same things. It's okay if you're there for moral support. How about you, Melissa?"

"Yep, I don't mind talking. Since Kate did so well, and Tori would like to be there to help, how about I go with Colt, and we'll switch off?"

Colt shrugged. "Sure. Works for me. We'll take one side of the street, and you girls take the other. We'll meet here at the car when we're done."

Kate and Tori stayed on the side where the grocery store was located, while Colt and Melissa crossed the road and went over the railroad tracks to start at a business a little north of the store.

Tori shuffled along behind Kate until Kate swiveled and stopped. "What's up?"

Tori ducked her head. "Sorry I'm being such a scaredy-cat."

"You are not. There's stuff I don't like to do, but it doesn't make me a scaredy-cat. Tell you what. You hand out the flyer, then give the people your nicest smile and pray. I'm so pumped about doing this now that I know nothing can go wrong. We're going to raise a ton of money and send a dozen kids to camp. You just see if we don't!"

Thirty minutes later, Kate wished she'd kept her silly prediction to herself. They'd talked to two more businesses. The owner wasn't at the first one, and the employee couldn't make any decisions. At the second business, the owner said the economy had been too bad, and he was sorry, but there was nothing he could do. When Kate asked if he'd consider a ten-dollar gift certificate, he shooed them out the door saying he was too busy to talk more. Maybe they could check back another time, but not today.

Kate and Tori met Colt and Melissa within a couple of minutes after they finished, and from the expression on both of their faces, it didn't look like they'd done much better.

Still, Colt held up an envelope and waved it in the air. "This isn't anything like what you got at the first store, but I guess it's better than nothing. The pizza place gave us coupons for twenty dollars' worth of pizzas. The owners weren't at the other two places."

Melissa sighed. "So what did you and Tori get? Another fifty dollars, I'll bet. At least someone is good at this. We probably should have had Kate talk to everyone."

Warmth rose in Kate's cheeks—not from embarrassment at the compliment but from guilt that she'd acted so excited about getting that first certificate and then bombed out so badly this time. "Naw. You did better than us. One owner wasn't there, and the other one said it's not in his budget." She avoided her mother's gaze. "You guys think maybe we should give up? We could give the grocery certificate back, and the pizza coupons you got."

Tori's eyes filled with tears. "But if we do that, what about Pete? The poor little guy won't get to go to camp."

Melissa crossed her arms over her chest. "No way am I giving up. This wasn't fun. In fact, one time it was downright humiliating when an employee laughed at me and Colt and said we were just kids who were probably trying to steal money from business owners and use it ourselves. But I want to keep going for Pete's sake."

Kate's mom cleared her throat. "Thanks, kids, for trying so hard. I don't want you to feel you have to do this. It *is* hard— I've worked fund-raisers in the past—and like Melissa said, it can be humiliating. But don't think that all the business owners you meet will be like that employee. I'm guessing he was young, right?"

Colt nodded. "Yeah, probably about nineteen or so."

"The people who matter are the owners or managers. And maybe what you need is a letter from an adult—like the owners of the Blue Ribbon Barn who are sponsoring this ride—stating that it's a legitimate fund-raiser and how the money will be put to use. We rushed into this without thinking of everything. But in spite of that, you did well. You have a fifty-dollar gift certificate and coupons for twenty dollars' worth of pizzas, and that's an awesome start. Let's have your dad draft and sign a letter, Kate, then you kids can try again. We could even design a simple website where people can check us out. Sound good?"

Kate nodded. "Sorry for being a baby and wanting to give up."

Melissa bumped her. "Hey, remember what a baby I was when I didn't want to go into Mrs. Maynard's spooky attic, and you held my hand and dragged me upstairs?"

Kate's pent-up breath whooshed out in relief. The more she got to know Melissa, the more she liked her. But it didn't hurt to tease a bit, when she had the chance. She looked Melissa squarely in the eyes. "Yep. I sure do remember that."

Melissa's smile faded, and Kate giggled. "And you're the coolest 'baby' I've ever met."

Melissa rolled her eyes. "Oh. Ha-ha."

"I'm kidding, Melissa. You aren't a baby at all, and it's awesome you're on our team! Now let's get back to the house and ask Dad to write a letter that'll convince every business owner in town to contribute to our cause. With Mom and Dad on our side, we can't lose."

Chapter Three

A week later, Kate and Tori waited in the office for Kate's mom to return, while Colt and Melissa answered questions and helped in the main area of the barn as people arrived to sign up for the trail ride.

Kate danced from one foot to the other, barely able to hold still. "This is so cool! I'm glad we got the ad in the paper in time and made all the calls to the barns and horse clubs. I can't believe we ended up with over a thousand dollars in prizes and gift certificates between the businesses in Odell, Hood River, and White Salmon. That was brilliant of you to think about going across the bridge to the Washington side."

Tori smiled. "You would have thought about it sooner or later. I'm so thankful our parents helped drive us around—even Melissa's mom. That kind of surprised me."

"Me too. Do you suppose she's noticing changes in Melissa's attitude? Maybe she's curious about what's going on."

"I sure hope so," Tori said. "From a couple of things Melissa said, she believes in God now, and she really wants to know more. We should pray for her mom."

"For sure." Kate turned as her mother entered the office. "Hey, Mom, we've got more entry money. A lot of people are paying in cash. Are you taking it to the bank today?"

"Not until just before five o'clock. I want to take as much as we can in one trip, rather than going two or three times a day. Since tomorrow is Saturday, I'm guessing we may have double the entries we do today. That money can go to the bank on Monday." She walked across the office and plucked an ornate box off the shelf, then took a tiny key from her pocket and undid the lock.

"That's beautiful." Tori's gaze fixed on the box. "Is it an antique? It looks really old. And I love the deep-blue-and-gold colors."

Kate's mom nodded. "Yes, it was my great-grandmother's box. I probably should use a regular cash box, but I didn't want to go buy one, and I already had this. It's been in my bedroom for years, and I never use it. It's more of an antique jewelry box—Great-Grandma got it as a wedding present—but I thought it would work well for the two or three days we need to store the entry fees."

Melissa stopped in the open doorway with Colt on her heels. "Wow! Cool box, Mrs. Ferris. It looks valuable."

Colt scratched his head. "It looks like a painted box to me. What's so special about it?"

Tori groaned. "Boys have no appreciation for the finer things of life."

He grinned. "Sure we do. Some of the finest things I can think of are desserts, long horseback rides, and going to amusement parks and hitting the wild rides. What's finer than that?"

Kate's mom laughed. "Works for me. But this box has been in my family for almost eighty years, so I consider it a treasure. And an antique dealer once offered me a nice sum of money for it, although I'd never part with it. Someday, when Kate gets married, I'll give it to her."

It was Kate's turn to groan. "Seriously, Mom? That might never happen. It's not like I have a boyfriend or even want one right now. Are you sure you want to use it as a cash box?"

Her mom nodded. "I'll keep it locked and in a cabinet when no one is in here." She lifted the lid, then tucked the cash inside the box. "Any of you kids collect more?"

"Yep." Kate extended her hand. "That's why Tori and I were waiting."

Colt did the same. "Melissa and I collected another thirty dollars. That was a great idea to let kids under twelve enter for half price."

Kate's mom placed the money inside and lowered the lid, then snapped the lock in place. "Thanks. You're all doing a super job."

A knock sounded at the door, and Kate turned. Mr. Abbington, the owner of a small café on the outskirts of Hood River, stood in the doorway. He was a short man with wire-rimmed glasses, and he kept pushing them up on his nose. "Sorry to interrupt." His gaze strayed to the box, and his eyes widened. "Lovely. I say, I need to get my son signed up for the trail ride. Can someone take care of that for me?"

"Certainly." Kate's mom set the box on the shelf. "Why don't you kids see if anyone else needs help, and if not, toss hay to the horses."

"Sure, Mom." Kate glanced at the man again as she left. She waited until she was out of earshot, then whispered to Melissa, "Isn't he one of the business owners who refused to donate?"

"Yep. I'm surprised he's here."

Colt stuck a piece of straw in his mouth. "Maybe he changed his mind. He might have felt bad about his attitude and decided to donate when his son said he wanted to enter."

Tori hunched a shoulder. "It's not like everyone has to donate, but if they're going to take part, it would be nice."

Kate stared at the open office door from across the arena. "Did you guys notice him staring at Mom's box? I'm glad she's taking the money to the bank."

Kate finished cleaning the last stall the next morning and heaved a sigh of relief. She'd gotten up an hour earlier to get the chores done before people started arriving, and it was a good thing she had. A car door slammed in the parking area. She stowed the pitchfork and wheelbarrow, then hurried to the open doors in time to see a car heading back toward the road.

"Hey, Tori." She walked out to meet her friend. "I'm glad it's you. How come you didn't ride your bike?"

"My mom had to run to town, so she said she'd drop me off and pick me up later, unless I want to walk home. Are Colt and Melissa coming?"

"Yeah. Melissa called this morning and said she'd be a little late, but Colt should be here any minute."

A bike turned off the road, and Colt pedaled across the gravel parking area, then skidded to a stop, spraying Kate and Tori with fine pebbles. "Oops. Sorry about that." But the mischievous twinkle in his eyes didn't look a bit sorry to Kate.

"Sure you are." She brushed off her jeans, which were already covered with bits of straw and dirt. "You turn up right after Tori and I get all the work done. Slacker." She turned and winked at Tori.

Her friend raised her chin in the air. "We've been slaving away for an hour while you were probably sleeping. And we've signed up another ten people without any help."

Colt's mouth fell open. "Seriously? Hey, I'm really sorry. I did kind of oversleep."

Kate burst into a laugh. "Gotcha. No one's been here to sign up yet, and Tori arrived a couple of minutes before you did. But I did get the stalls cleaned and the horses fed. Thankfully most of the horses are out to pasture, so I only had to clean two stalls. Not a biggie."

He walked beside them back to the barn. "So is your mom worried about the money box after you told her how Mr. Abbington was eyeing it?"

"She thought we were imagining things and said he's a reputable businessman. Nothing happened yesterday, but she did take the box into the house for the night. She finished here too late to get to the bank."

Tori tilted her head. "So it's back in the office for the day?"

"Yes. Mom puts it in a cabinet, so she's not worried about it. Besides, everybody knows this is a charity event. No way would anyone steal our money."

A car pulled in as they were almost to the barn door, and three college-age kids got out. One of them waved. "Is this the right place for the trail-ride scavenger hunt?"

"Sure is." Kate pointed inside the barn. "The office is half-way down the alleyway. I'll grab entry forms for you, and you can pay with cash or a check."

One of the boys pulled out his wallet. "Cash is fine. We heard there's a lot of prizes, and that the money is going to a good cause."

The girl who'd gotten out of the car second nodded. "I have an autistic sister. She's too old for the camp now, but she would have loved it when she was younger."

Kate's insides warmed. "My little brother is only six, and we're hoping he might get to go to the day camp this year. He's why we thought about doing this in the first place."

They all walked into the barn together, and Kate waved toward the office. "The door is open. If you want to fill out the forms inside, you can, or you can bring them back later."

The girl smiled. "Gordon and I are the only ones riding. We'll fill the forms out now." She turned her head and looked at the outer door. "Sounds like you've got more people coming."

A man and a young girl walked in. "Is this where we get the entry form for the scavenger hunt? I need to leave my daughter so she can look over the barn and find out what she has to do, then I'll pick her up in thirty minutes or so. I'm in a hurry. Could you get me a form right away?" His tone was sharp and almost pushy, and Kate's hackles rose.

Colt eased forward, standing in front of the girls. "Sure. But these people were first, so you'll have to wait your turn, Mr. …?"

"Creighton. I don't have time to wait. I'm sure they won't mind letting me go first. I need to get to an appointment in town."

Colt drew in a breath, but the girl held up her hand. "It's fine. We're not in a hurry."

The boy who'd been silent the entire time stepped forward. "It's not okay with me, Lisa. We were here first."

Lisa waved her hand. "Relax, Jerry. I plan to fill my form out here. Besides, I want time to talk to these guys about the ride. Go ahead and help him first."

Tori looked from Lisa to the man who'd just arrived. "When you're finished, maybe I can answer your questions, or I can take you to see Mrs. Ferris. Would that work?"

"Sure." Lisa glanced around. "It's pretty crowded in here. How about we step outside and I'll finish this, then you can take me to the lady in charge."

Tori nodded and followed the three students out of the office.

Colt shot the man a hard look, then waved Kate toward the office. They both went in and grabbed a few forms, leaving the door open. When they stepped out into the alleyway, Kate noticed Jerry and Mr. Creighton looking over their heads—right toward the antique box.

As Kate gestured for the man and his daughter to come inside, he followed and smiled, but somehow it didn't feel real. "Thank you, young lady. As I said, I'll be back soon."

"Dad, I'd rather wait in the car than stay here." The girl, who appeared to be a couple of years younger than Kate and her friends, spoke in a whining tone.

"Fine. Come along then. We'll come back as soon as we're able, if you're sure you want to take part in this ride."

She sighed dramatically. "There's nothing else to do this summer, and I'd like to win the raft trip down the White Salmon River. My friends would think I was so cool if I had a trip for four and invited three of them to come." She took the form Kate handed her and exited the office with her father.

Melissa rolled her eyes, and Kate could tell exactly what she was thinking. Melissa had spent years trying to buy the friendship of several of the girls at their school, only to be dumped when they found out her father had left the family, disappearing with most of their money and leaving her and her mother practically broke.

Someone tapped Kate from behind, and she pivoted. "Oh, hi, Mr. Wallace."

Their neighbor, a man who was usually somewhat of a recluse, stood with his arms crossed and glowering. "When is all this traffic going to slow down?" He stepped around Kate and into the open doorway. "Where's your mother?" His gaze scanned the room, and he paused. "That's an antique jewelry box." His voice softened. "My grandmother had one very similar, even down to the jeweled enamel finish. May I hold it?" He took another step into the room, his face eager.

Kate rushed around him and planted herself in front of him, her heart pounding. "No sir, Mr. Wallace. I'm afraid not. Mom doesn't want anyone to touch it. We're keeping the entry fees in there." She clamped her lips shut, wishing she could take back what she'd said. Mom was so careful to open the box and stash the money inside only when no one was around, and now several people had seen the box. "This is our last day for entries, and things should get a lot quieter. I'm so sorry it's been a bother."

He kept his eyes fixed on the box. "No bother at all. If your mother ever wants to part with her box, tell her to give me first chance. I'd love to purchase it."

Kate shook her head. "She won't. It was a gift from her great-grandmother, and she'll be taking it into the house this evening as soon as we're done."

"I see." He appeared to have difficulty removing his gaze from the box but backed toward the door, then swiveled and reached for the knob. "Have a good day then. Good-bye." He cast one more glance over his shoulder, then strode down the alleyway toward the exit.

The rest of the day sped by, and Kate didn't see the man or his daughter come back with the entry form, but she'd been so busy exercising Capri, helping to feed the horses, and answering questions that they could easily have come and gone without her noticing. More than one person had questioned why it cost twenty dollars to take part in the trail ride. Kate's mom had been gracious and sweet, explaining to every person that it was a benefit, and that the prizes were nicer than what was typically found in scavenger hunts.

Tori leaned on a post and blew out her breath. "Whew. I'm tired! But it's been a great day. At least this part is over."

Kate nodded. "Mom and Dad didn't want to have to deal with this on Sunday. And isn't it cool that three more business owners made donations?"

Colt grinned. "Even more cool that two of them were ones we visited in Odell who said no. I guess they felt left out when word started spreading about all the businesses that contributed."

Kate tipped her head. "And that wouldn't have happened if you hadn't thought of putting an ad in the *Hood River News* telling about the ride and listing all the businesses that donated."

"I wonder …" Tori's voice trailed off as Kate's mom rushed out of the office and then looked up and down the alleyway.

"What's wrong, Mom? Did you need something?" Kate took a step toward her, then noticed her pale face. A sense of dread hit.

"My box is gone. It was there an hour or two ago, the last time I put money in it. It's been so quiet the past hour that I forgot all about it. Did one of you take it to the house?"

They all looked at one another, then slowly shook their heads. Tori grabbed Kate's arm. "Did someone steal it? With all of our money inside?"

Her mother's lips trembled. "By the time I helped the last person yesterday, I was so tired, I didn't think about taking the money out. And this morning I was in a rush, so I brought it back to the office without emptying it first. The box with all of our money is gone."

Chapter Four

The next couple of hours dragged as Kate and her friends helped her mom hunt through the entire barn in case someone had moved the box. When nothing turned up, Nan Ferris went into the house to start dinner and check on Pete, since his tutor had just gone home.

Kate plunked down on a bale of straw outside one of the stalls as each of her friends found a place to sit. "Who could have taken Mom's box, and how did they get it out of the barn without someone seeing them?"

Melissa clenched her fists. "I'd like to get my hands on the person who took that money. It's really rotten stealing something that will benefit kids!"

Colt's normally tranquil expression had turned angry. "No kidding! All that work with nothing to show for it."

Tori's face crumpled as if she might cry. "We worked so hard. So do we give back all the donations and cancel the ride?

This was the final day people could enter, and we don't have any of the money."

Kate sighed. "We can't cancel. It won't matter to the people who paid to enter the scavenger hunt that someone took the money. Well, it might matter to them, but it's not their problem. They entered expecting to take part and hoping to win stuff. If we can't give their money back, then we can't cancel the ride."

Tori groaned. "I didn't think of that. So we'll have to scramble to get things ready and not get anything out of it? Won't the business owners be mad if we don't have a fund for the kids? That's the reason most of them donated."

Colt thumped his boot heel against the bale of straw he was sitting on. "We've got to think of something we can do to get that money back and catch the person who took it."

Melissa tucked a blonde strand of hair behind her ear. "Silly, we can't catch someone after he's already taken the box and gone. There's nothing more for him to steal."

Silence fell over the group as they took in what she'd said. Then Kate sat up a little straighter. "But what if the thief doesn't know he got all the money? What if we open the trail ride to more entries for another couple of days—like Monday and Tuesday? We could put the word out that we want to be fair and not leave anyone out. You know, call the Pony Club leader, the 4-H club leaders, and other barns and ask them to spread the news. That might get the thief to come back in the hope of stealing more money."

"Okay …" Colt frowned. "But it's not like we can station someone at the door of the office, and there's no place to hide inside."

Kate slumped. His words made sense. "Right. I hadn't thought that far."

Melissa brightened. "Maybe we could keep the office door shut and have someone hang around all day, then make a big deal about having to be gone in the evening. If the thief thinks the barn won't be guarded, he might come back later."

Tori gave a slow nod, her brow puckered. "Good. But how do we catch him?"

Colt grinned. "Now that's something a guy can figure out. Set a trap, of course."

The girls leaned forward.

"What kind?" Kate asked.

"We turn on a webcam and have it pointed at the door, or we could put a bucket of paint over the inside of the office door so it'll dump on the thief when he goes in. We could hide up in the hayloft above the alleyway so we can peek over the edge and watch."

Melissa waved her hand. "Or we could do all of that at the same time, right?"

Colt's eyes widened. "Yeah. Great idea, Melissa! Let's go catch that thief."

Kate barely dragged through the day on Sunday. She attended church with her family and sat by Tori, but she had a hard time keeping her mind on the service. She'd wanted all three of her friends to come over that afternoon, but Mom and Dad said there'd been enough excitement lately, and it was time for her to rest and spend time with Pete. That didn't bother her, since she loved her little brother, but she hoped she and her friends would have enough time to plan what they needed to do to catch the thief.

After playing video games with Pete for an hour and cleaning her room, she approached her mother again. "How about if only Tori comes over? Please, Mom? I cleaned my room and played games with Pete. She and I can take turns reading *Pete's Dragon* to him later if he wants us to. And we'll be quiet so you and Dad can rest." She started to walk away, then pivoted. "Have you heard any more from the police?"

Mom sighed. "They said it's going to be very difficult to find the box. The office has had so many people in it that fingerprints are out. They asked questions and took notes, but they aren't very hopeful. As to having Tori over, I don't see why not. I appreciate your offer to entertain Pete. Dad and I would like a few minutes alone this afternoon. Go ahead and call her."

"All right!" Kate raced to the phone. At least she and Tori could do a little planning. Maybe they could even call Colt and Melissa later and tell them what they'd come up with, then ask them to work on ideas so they could have a solid plan tomorrow.

"Kate." Her mom's voice halted her before she could dial. "You can call Colt and Melissa as well. Don't ask them to come over, but if the four of you can split up the barns and riding clubs in the Gorge and make sure they've all been notified of the extension for entering, that would be a big help. I'm tired."

Kate nodded. "Sure, Mom." She grinned as she dialed Tori's number, happy that her mother had given her a good reason to call the rest of her friends.

Tori arrived on her bike thirty minutes later. She skidded to a stop by the front door, where Kate waited. "Hey. I'm glad you called. I wasn't sure if your mom and dad would want company after everything you guys have been through." She parked her bike, then headed up the steps.

Kate stood aside as her friend entered the house. "We have an hour to talk and make calls, then we need to read to Pete, if that's okay with you."

"Sure. I love Pete. Who are we calling?"

Kate filled her in on her mother's request. "I already told Colt and Melissa, and they took most of the list. We'll talk to the two clubs that are left. Then we can talk about plans for our sting operation."

Tori stared at Kate. "Huh? Sting?"

Kate grinned. "You know—like the cops do when they want to catch a bad guy. We're going to set up something that will make the thief want to come back and try again." She rubbed her hands together. "This is gonna be fun."

Early the next morning, Kate ran to the barn, hoping Tori would arrive in the next half hour. She slid to a stop and stared. "Tori! I can't believe you beat me!"

"I couldn't sleep, and you said to get here early, so I did."

"Yeah, but it's six thirty! I figured you'd come closer to seven. I was going to get the horses fed and the two stalls cleaned so we'd be ready when Colt and Melissa arrive."

"We'll get done faster if we do it together."

Kate smiled as warmth rushed through her. "Right." It sure was good to have a close friend.

In no time they finished up and then heard Colt's cheerful whistle outside. He sauntered into the barn carrying a bottle of water, with Melissa on his heels. "Hey, guys. You just starting?"

"The stalls are done. Glad you're both here so we can get some work done for our sting before people arrive."

Melissa held up a lightweight laptop. "It's got a great webcam. We can set it up in the hayloft and point it right at the office door."

"Cool." Tori looked at Colt. "Did you bring the paint?"

He grabbed a piece of straw from a nearby bale. "I got to thinking about that. If we put it above the door inside the office and the thief steps in, it's going to dump paint all over the stuff in the office, not just on the person."

Kate and Melissa groaned at the same time. "Right." Kate sank onto a nearby bale. "I can't believe we didn't think of that while we were planning. Now what?"

He held up his finger, then swiveled and walked outside. He returned in a minute carrying a plastic pail. "Watch." He grabbed a manure fork, then turned and pushed open a stall door. "Not much left in here, but it'll do for a demo."

He placed a few pieces of horse droppings in the bucket, then reached for the water bottle he'd set on the bale. He uncapped the bottle and poured water into the bucket, then plucked a stick from his pocket, dipped it into the bucket, and stirred. "Voilà!

Soupy horse droppings! Stinky and sloppy. It's easier to clean up than paint, and if we don't fill it full, it'll mostly get on the person who walks under it. What do you think? It should be enough to slow him down as he runs out the door, and if we're lucky, it'll be on his face and he won't be able to see well enough to run. We should be able to catch him. All we have to do is follow the smell."

Kate laughed. "Brilliant. But we can't set that up while people are signing up for the ride. And if we're up in the loft watching later, why the webcam?"

Melissa gave a sheepish grin. "It's for tonight, in case we fall asleep."

Tori startled. "You think we'll have to stay out here all night? I'm not sure my parents will go for that." She settled on one of the straw bales and waved for the others to sit as well.

Melissa shrugged. "I already told my mom I'm spending the night with Kate so I can help with the trail-ride sign-ups this afternoon and early tomorrow. She didn't care."

Kate glanced at Tori. "What do you think?"

"I don't think Mom will care if I spend the night, as long as it's okay with your parents. But what about Colt?"

He frowned. "What about me?"

Tori raised one brow. "Won't your parents think it's weird if you ask to spend the night at a girl's house?"

"Nope, I already told them you needed help with the ride, so I was going to spend the night in the loft. I knew we'd have to have someone out here tonight watching the webcam."

"Perfect," Kate said. "That's the honest truth. We need your help, and you'll be sleeping in the loft."

He brightened. "And if we catch the guy early, you girls will be in the house, and I'll be out here in my sleeping bag watching old Westerns on the laptop and eating popcorn." He pumped his fist in the air. "Yeah! It doesn't get much better than that."

Melissa rolled her eyes. "Have I ever mentioned how weird boys are?"

Tori grinned. "Yep. But it doesn't hurt to say it again."

"Whatever." Colt squared his shoulders. "Hey, did you make a list of the people who were eyeing the box? How are we going to make sure they come again?"

"That's the hard part," Kate said. "There were several people we saw looking at Mom's box or who made comments about it. One was Mr. Wallace, our neighbor who lives just down the road. He's kind of a cranky old man, but he sure cheered up after he saw Mom's box. I figured we'd call and apologize that people will still be coming today, since we want to make more money."

Tori kicked her foot against a straw bale. "Then there was the other man who didn't want to wait, and he couldn't take his eyes off that box. He and his daughter took a form, and he said he'd bring it back later, but none of us saw him." She turned to Melissa. "Did you check to make sure he brought the entry form back? What do we say to him?"

Melissa exhaled. "Yeah, I found his daughter's entry. Maybe we could call him and let him know we're opening it again, in case his daughter has a friend who wants to come."

"Great," Kate said. "There were some college kids too, and a couple of others I thought acted suspicious when they were in the office—like Mr. Abbington the first day. That cash box was on my mind all day after Mr. Wallace said he wanted to buy it."

"He what?" Tori squeaked the last word. "Maybe we should call the police and ask them to search his house."

Colt shook his head. "We don't have any proof. By the way, Kate, did your parents call the police to report the theft? They should."

She nodded. "They did, but they're worried about it ending up in the paper and people getting upset that the ride might not take place. So Dad told the police to keep an eye open, but he said he didn't want to file an official report yet. We definitely don't want the thief to get spooked and not come again. Besides, the police didn't think there was much chance of catching the person, since there were a few dozen people in and out of here over those two days."

Silence fell over the group. Finally Kate pushed to her feet. "Let's get that laptop up to the loft and pointed at the office door. Colt, did you bring a sleeping bag?"

"Yep. Unlike you girls, I thought ahead." He winked. "*Now* try to tell me boys are weird or not smarter than girls."

Melissa smirked. "We don't have to—we'll take a vote and win. But seriously, Colt. That's a cool idea about the bucket of manure. Now we need to spread the word and hope the thief takes the bait."

Kate shivered. "And pray he didn't already spend our money and ditch the box. That would be a total catastrophe!"

Chapter Five

Kate sighed with relief. Her parents had given them permission to take popcorn and sodas up to the loft for the evening. She propped herself on her elbows and looked at her friends. "We had an okay day, I guess. Only a half-dozen entries, but at least we got word out to all the people who are on our suspect list."

Colt tossed buttered popcorn into his mouth and chewed, then asked, "Did you see any of them today? I never got a look at the ones you were talking about."

Tori shook her head. "I didn't, but I wasn't with Kate every minute. We had lessons on top of everything else, and I won't miss a chance to ride Starlight." She grinned. "I still can't believe he's mine. Well, mine and Mrs. Maynard's. He's such an awesome horse."

Melissa took a sip of her soda. "That was pretty cool of Mrs. Maynard to give him to you. How often does she come to visit?

I've been over to see her once in the past week, but with this event going on, I've been busy."

"She comes at least twice a week to see Starlight. He's excited when she arrives—she always gives him a hug and carrots." Tori giggled. "I'm not sure which he likes best, but I kind of think he's partial to the carrots." She sobered. "But you're right. I still have to pinch myself to believe he's mine. Mrs. Maynard even told me she put me in her will—that if she dies before Starlight does, she's leaving a small fund to pay for his hay and board the rest of his life. I'll have to take care of shoes and shots and stuff, but that's fine. I told her I'd pay for all of that now, but she said I'm doing enough taking care of him and exercising him."

"Wow! I wish I had someone doing that for me." Melissa crinkled her forehead. "I've been kind of worried lately." She pressed her lips together and stopped.

Kate touched Melissa's arm. "What's up? We won't make fun or tease you."

"I know." Melissa blinked her eyes rapidly. "You guys have been cool since you found out my mom is broke—not like the other people who pretended to be my friends. My mom told me she's not sure how much longer she can pay Mocha's expenses."

Colt pushed the popcorn bowl aside. "Kate, did you say recently that your mom was talking about hiring part-time help for the barn? Is it something Melissa could do, even for the rest of the summer? You know, pay off her board and save their cash for the winter." He smiled at Melissa. "That is, if you'd be willing to work."

She blew out a hard breath. "That would be awesome!" She stared down at her clenched hands. "I've even been praying about it lately, but I didn't think God would care enough to do anything about it."

"Seriously?" Kate sat up. "Wow! God could be answering your prayer and Mom's at the same time. She was thinking about running an ad. The barn is almost full now, and it's more work than she and I can do on our own. It'll be easier during the school year with Pete going to his class a few hours every day, but summer is rough. Want me to ask her?"

Melissa shook her head. "Thanks, but if I want the job, it's up to me to talk to her. Thank you both for mentioning it. It's pretty cool that God actually answered."

Colt propped his feet on a pile of hay and leaned his back against a bale. "The webcam's set up, and we'll turn it on if we start getting sleepy, but what now? Just sit and hope someone shows up? Oh, and I got the bucket of horse poop mixed with a little water set on a tiny shelf above the door in the office. If the door opens, it's rigged to pull the pail over and dump the contents."

"Way to go!" Kate smacked her hands together. "There's no way the thief can sneak in and get back out without us knowing it, even if we do go to sleep. We'll hear the noise and wake up."

Tori grinned. "I brought a cowbell over that I borrowed from a friend of my dad's and set it inside the door too. That's the first thing the person's foot will hit, and it's loud."

Melissa giggled. "How did you manage that without getting the bucket of manure on your head?"

"I did it this evening at the same time Colt set his trap."

"We'd better whisper from now on. No one would sneak into the office in the daylight, but it's almost dark." Kate peered over the side of the loft. "And maybe scoot back a bit so we can't be seen from the alleyway."

An hour passed with whispers getting fewer and yawns becoming more frequent. Melissa turned on the webcam. "Just in case."

"Right." Colt nodded. "I was thinking I might shut my eyes for a minute or two. Then I'll probably wake up again and keep watch. You girls can rest if you want to."

Kate shook her head. "I'm too wound up. But the rest of you go ahead."

Tori frowned. "Are you sure?"

"Yep. No way will I sleep."

Tori sighed. "I am a little sleepy. Wake me up after a bit, and I'll keep you company."

"Sounds good."

Kate settled deeper into the pile of hay where she'd spread a blanket, envying Colt with his sleeping bag. She, Tori, and Melissa should probably go inside soon, but she hated leaving when nothing had happened yet. It would be awful if they came out in the morning and found the traps hadn't worked and the webcam had stopped running. What if the thief returned, and they missed him?

She rubbed her eyes and yawned. Maybe it wouldn't hurt if she simply rested her eyes. She shifted to a sitting position against a bale. No way would she go to sleep sitting up.

Her eyes drifted shut …

Sometime later, a loud yell and a thud jerked Kate upright. "What? Who?"

Tori thrashed on the blanket next to her, still asleep, batting at some imaginary thing in the air.

Colt rolled to a sitting position, then reached over and shook Melissa's shoulder. "Hey. Wake up. Somebody's downstairs." He lowered his voice. "I think he stumbled into our trap. Hear that? It's the cowbell Tori planted. Come on! We need to catch him before he gets away."

Kate woke Tori and looked around. The lights in the barn were mostly out, with only one at the entrance and one in the alleyway a few yards from the office door. Who had come in and turned off the lights while they slept? The thief? Was he thrashing on the office floor in horse manure? She scrambled to her feet and looked at Melissa. "Should we call the police?"

Melissa hesitated. "I'm not sure. Maybe we should run in and get your parents."

Colt shook his head. "The thief could get away by the time we do that." He snatched a rope hanging on a post nail. "I brought this in case we needed it. We'll tie him up and let your dad call the cops." He slung the coil of rope over his shoulder, then hurried down the ladder to the floor below.

Kate heard mumbling and grunts coming from inside the office. She scrambled down the ladder after Tori and Melissa, then stopped next to her three friends. "It's definitely a man. What if there's more than one?" She shivered and rubbed her hands up and down her arms. "Are you sure we shouldn't call the police?"

Colt kept walking. "It might take all of us to tackle the robber."

Tori rocked on her toes. "What if he has a gun? I want to get Mr. Ferris."

Colt grabbed a shovel leaning against a stall door. "Come on. I'll bash him over the head with this if I have to, and we can tie him up. It'll be okay, Tori. As soon as we know we have him, you run get Mr. Ferris."

She nodded. "Okay, I guess." But Kate could tell she wasn't convinced.

The four of them crept toward the door, with Colt leading the way. He handed the rope to Kate, who followed close behind; then he raised the shovel above his head. "Shhh. Careful now." He eased open the office door. "Come out with your hands up. We have you surrounded!"

Chapter Six

The door flew the rest of the way open, and a man stood there. The light of the office streamed out the doorway, illuminating Kate and her friends but keeping his face in shadow. One thing Kate could tell was he didn't smell very good.

He took a step forward, and they all backed up. "What do you mean put my hands up? Kate, what is the meaning of this mess?" He pointed to his shoulders, where most of the sloppy manure had landed.

Kate gasped. She recognized the voice immediately, even if she couldn't see his face. "Dad? What are you doing out here?" She stepped back as far as she could and bumped into either Tori or Melissa. "Sorry." She wrinkled her nose. "You smell pretty bad, Dad."

"You think?" He stepped into the light of the alleyway. Wet manure clung to his shirt front and dotted his hair. He reached down to rub his ankle, and a glob of manure fell out of his hair and hit the floor.

He stood again, then glared as he crossed his arms. "Who did this and why? When that stuff landed on me, I stumbled forward and almost broke my ankle on something big and metal, and it was all I could do not to land on the floor."

Now that Kate could see her dad, she could barely contain her giggles. She felt bad, but he looked *so* funny standing there dripping in wet horse poop! "Wow. You *are* a mess." Then she sobered, realizing she and her friends could be in big trouble.

The outer door on the house side of the barn opened wider, and Kate's mom stepped into the dim light. She flipped the main switch, and every alleyway light and arena light sprang to life. "John? You've been out here a long time. Is everything all right?" She walked toward them, then stopped a yard or so away. "What in the world?"

"That's what I'd like to know." He turned a stern gaze on Kate, letting it linger there for what felt like an eternity. "Are you trying not to laugh at me, young lady?"

"Uh …" She pressed her lips together hard. "Uh …" She couldn't help it. A giggle escaped. "You do look kinda funny."

Tori gasped behind her. "Kate!"

Colt glanced from Kate to her father and back, then chuckled. "Yep. He kinda does. Guess he's not our thief, though, so we went to all that work for nothing." He killed his grin. "We're really sorry, Mr. Ferris. We were trying to catch the robber."

Kate's mother's mouth dropped open. "Now that doesn't make a bit of sense. Why would the person who stole my box come back again?"

Kate kicked at a piece of manure that had dropped from her father's shoulder. "Well, you see … that's why we wanted to make those calls and tell people we were going to extend the entry period for another two days. We called everyone we thought might be suspects, as well as the barns and horse clubs."

Kate's mom stepped into the nearby tack room, then came out with a towel. "Suspects?" She handed her husband the towel. "Here. Why don't you see how much of that you can wipe off? Or better yet, how about you rinse off in the wash rack here in the barn. Then you can shower in the house, and we'll hear the rest of the story." She turned to Kate. "And while he's doing that, I want the four of you to do the best you can cleaning up the mess in the office. You'll have to give it another scrubbing tomorrow."

Twenty minutes later they all met in the kitchen and gathered around the table, waiting for the hot chocolate to heat and Kate's dad to return from his shower. The mugs and her dad arrived at the same time, and he settled into his chair with a grateful sigh. "This sure smells a lot better than I did. I'm not sure my clothes will ever be the same."

"I'm really sorry, Dad. We didn't mean to hurt or scare you, or make you stink." Kate giggled again. "But I do wish I'd had a camera when you stepped into the light."

"The camera!" Melissa exclaimed. "The webcam is probably still running, if the laptop battery isn't dead by now. It's all recorded."

Kate's dad groaned, and her mom laughed. "Now there's a video Kate can save to show her kids someday—their grandfather covered in horse poop while they all stand around thinking they caught a thief."

Kate's dad shook his head, but he managed a grin. "Not happening, Nan. Now let's get to the bottom of this. You said you hoped the thief would get word you'd extended the entry days so he'd come back and try again? But what's this I heard about suspects? How did you come up with that idea?"

Kate plunged into the story. "Tori and I noticed more than one person who eyed that box or asked questions about it. Our neighbor up the road even said he wants to buy it if Mom sells it. You should have seen the look on his face when he saw it. So we called those people to let them know what we were doing—and it might have worked if you hadn't stumbled into the trap first."

She ducked her head. "Not that it's your fault or anything. We should have told you what we were doing, but we figured you wouldn't think it was safe for us to stay in the barn and keep watch. But all we caught was you, and we never saw anyone else, so I guess it was a dumb idea."

Tori raised her hand. "What made you come out to the office?"

Kate's mom took a sip of her cocoa. She set it down, then waved her hand in front of her mouth. "Hot! I'll answer that question. It's my fault your dad stumbled into your trap. I was going to come check on you, since it was nearing your bedtime, but I was too tired to get out of my easy chair. I also wanted to see how many entries we ended up with. I brought the metal cash box Dad got for me into the house today, but I left the entry forms on the desk in the office. Your father offered to go get them." She reached across the table and patted his hand. "Now he probably wishes he hadn't."

He grinned. "Now that I'm clean, I have a whole new outlook. A lot worse happened to me in the Marine Corps, let me tell you. I saw you kids were asleep, and I hated to wake you, so I turned off a couple of lights, then headed to the office to search for the papers. I planned to let Colt sleep and wake you girls when I came out. It was a shock when the bucket of manure landed on me. I'm thankful you used a small plastic pail instead of a metal bucket." He made a face. "I'll live. Although my toes and ankle still hurt where I smacked my foot against a big brass bell. Where'd that thing come from, anyway?"

Tori averted her gaze. "It's the biggest cowbell made, according to a friend of my dad who collects them. We hoped the thief would trip over it and get tangled in the cowbell rope if the manure trap didn't catch him. Now I feel terrible that I thought of it."

His chuckle turned into an outright laugh. "Our quiet, kind Tori has a cunning side that we've never seen. Interesting. But don't worry about it. You're forgiven, and my toes aren't broken." He tweaked a strand of her hair.

Kate laced her fingers around her mug. "So are we busted? Are you guys mad at us?"

Her parents exchanged a silent look. Then her mom gave a slight nod and settled back in her chair. "This one is all yours, John."

He smiled. "You aren't busted this time, because you were trying to do something good. As much as I'd like to be mad at you, I have to admit I did worse when I was a kid. Not that it makes it right for you not to bring us in on your plans, but I get it."

Kate slumped. "Thanks, Dad."

"Hold it." He held up his hand. "You aren't getting off that easily. I expect the four of you to clean that office from top to bottom. Not a bit of manure had better be in there by noon tomorrow, and I expect it to smell fresh and clean when you finish."

Colt looked at the girls, and they all nodded.

"Do you want us to finish it now?" Kate asked.

"No. You need to get some sleep, and so do your mother and I. It's late, and I have to work tomorrow. Colt, instead of you bunking in the barn loft, how about you go shut off that webcam and bring your sleeping bag into the living room? We have an extra pillow, and you can sack out on the couch."

"Sounds good, sir. I'll grab everything now." He pushed his chair back, then stood.

"Not alone, you won't." Kate's dad stood as well. "We don't know if that thief is still on the loose. On second thought, get your sleeping bag, and let's leave the webcam running. You never know—your idea might not have been dumb after all."

Chapter Seven

As soon as Kate and her friends woke in the morning, they raced to the barn and brought back the laptop. Her dad had run an extension cord to an outlet the night before so the laptop wouldn't have to run on battery power. Kate could hardly wait to check the footage of the rest of the night.

They went through hours of video with absolutely nothing happening, other than the event with her father. It was the first time Kate's mom had seen it, and Kate was certain her mother was working to contain a grin, if not a laugh, at the sight of Kate's dad walking out of the office into the light.

Kate sighed. "Looks like we didn't catch anybody. Now what?" She gazed at her parents and her three friends, who were all finishing up their eggs and toast.

Colt tipped his head to the side. "Dunno. I'm not sure there's much we can do. What do you think, Mrs. Ferris?"

"I think it's time to tell the newspaper—ask them to write an article and appeal to the person who stole the box. Let him know how important this event is, and that it will hurt disabled children who can't attend camp if that money isn't returned. We'll say we won't press charges if it's returned—that the person can even do it anonymously. What do you all think?"

Silence settled over the table. Melissa's face puckered in thought, Colt drummed his fingers against the tabletop, and Kate's dad rubbed his chin.

Tori yawned, then blushed. "Sorry. I think it's a good idea. Maybe it will make the person who took the box feel bad, and he'll return it. Especially if he knows he can do it without being questioned. I mean, he could leave it on your doorstep, right? It's not like he has to hand it to you in person."

Kate shook her head. "Not with Rufus around. He'd wake us all up barking if the thief tried it at night—but we do keep Rufus tied up when boarders come to ride. That's why I made sure he was in the house last night, so he wouldn't scare off the thief if he came back. But what makes you think the money isn't spent by now, Mom?"

"I don't know. Maybe it's wishful thinking, but I believe we need to at least try."

Kate's dad thumped the table with the flat of his palm. "Then I say do it. Today is the paper's deadline, so you'd better call it in right away. I'll let the police know what we've decided and about not pressing charges if the box and money are returned."

Colt narrowed his eyes. "I'm no Internet expert, but maybe we should put it out on the web somewhere as well."

Melissa straightened. "I can do that. My mom has several social-media accounts. I'll ask if she'll post our statement on those sites as well. Hopefully the person who took the box will see it and contact us."

Kate shook her head. "I'm not trying to have a bad attitude, but I'm not gonna count on it happening."

Tori grabbed Kate's hand. "Then we need to pray that it does. How many times since you moved here have we seen God do awesome stuff for us?"

Kate hung her head for a second, then raised it, ashamed that she'd let doubt and fear take over. "You're right. Tons of times. I have Capri and you have Starlight because of God's help, and Melissa's going to get a job at our barn, and—" She sucked in a hard breath when she saw Melissa's mouth drop open. "Oops. Sorry. I wasn't supposed to say that."

Kate's mother smiled. "Melissa, are you willing to work for us? If so, I'm thrilled! I've been praying that God would send us more help, even just for the summer. But I don't want Kate to back you into a corner if it's not your idea. It's fine if you want to say no."

"No!" Melissa clenched her fingers into fists. "I mean, yes! I don't want to say no, and yes, I do want a job. That would be awesome! Thank you."

Kate's mom nodded. "I'm thrilled you're willing to work for us. We'll talk over the hours and pay later, but right now I think we'd better figure out what we're going to tell the paper. We have a new group of students coming in for lessons this week. Let's keep telling people about what happened and hope they'll spread the word to their friends. Maybe the thief will hear and decide to come forward—whether because he reads the article or hears about it from someone. We'll cover all our bases and leave the rest up to God. Agreed?"

"Agreed." Kate echoed her mom, but she still doubted they'd ever see that money again. God cared, she knew that, and He'd answered prayer a lot of times, but they were dealing with someone who obviously didn't love God or believe in Him, or he wouldn't have stolen their box. At this point, it was pretty hard to trust the thief would have a change of heart and do anything good. It looked as if they'd be stuck trying to make up for the loss of the entry fees on their own.

The article came out in the paper two days later, on Thursday, and in spite of Kate's reluctance to believe anyone would come forward, she found herself listening for the phone and watching the road. The new group of students was starting in an hour, and Kate wanted to be there to watch—and talk to as many as she could in hopes that someone would have a suggestion or help to spread the word. Besides, it was a jumping lesson at a higher level than she'd been allowed to take part in, and she knew she'd learn something if she paid attention.

Tori and Melissa met her at the barn. Tori grinned at Melissa. "I'm glad it's you taking this lesson and not me. I'd sail right over Starlight's head if I tried to take him over one of those jumps."

Melissa smiled. "Not if you worked him up to it. Do you know if Mrs. Maynard ever used him for jumping?"

Tori shook her head. "She didn't. She said it never interested her. In fact, he was mostly ridden Western, but he's doing great at basic English riding. We're learning together."

Kate moved alongside the two girls in front of Melissa's stall, where Mocha was in cross ties. "He's looking really good. I'm glad his leg is all healed, and he's able to jump again. Do you plan to participate in any more shows this summer?"

"I doubt it. We don't have the money now." Melissa shrugged. "It's okay. I'm good with it. I mean, I'm disappointed, but I'm not going to complain."

Kate's eyes widened. This was a different Melissa from the one they'd met when she first came to the barn. "But you qualified for regionals at that last show. You'll go to that, right?"

"Dunno. Maybe if I can save enough money from working here, but paying for Mocha's board is the most important thing right now. I don't want to lose him. We sold the trailer, so I'd have to pay someone to haul Mocha, or find someone going who's willing to let us ride along. The entry fees aren't cheap either. I qualified for two classes, but at this point I'm not counting on it."

Tori's dark eyes appeared sad. "That's a bummer that you might not be able to go. I wish there was something we could do to help."

"You're doing enough by being my friends." Melissa smiled at Kate. "And offering to let me work here part-time. Besides, right now we need to concentrate on finding the money for the kids' camp expenses and putting the scavenger hunt together. When are you going to start working on the clues? Or are you having someone else do that?"

Kate leaned against a post. "Mom said she and two of the horse-club leaders could help us come up with some of the clues, but we'll be hiding all the items that riders will search for."

Tori blinked. "Why can't we take part in the hunt like everybody else?"

"You can, but I can't. Our barn is sponsoring it, and I'm going to help hide the items, so it wouldn't be fair if I hunt. But you and Melissa and Colt can. I don't want you to miss out on the fun."

Tori frowned. "Does that mean you won't even go on the ride?"

"I'll go, but I'll tag along behind and help make sure everything's going smoothly. I want you guys to do it, though. You might win some awesome stuff!"

Melissa raised her chin in determination. "No can do. I work for the barn now, so it wouldn't look right if I win anything. I'll ride with you, if that's okay."

A step sounded on the wood floor behind them, and they turned. Colt stood with an easy posture. "Count me in on tagging along with you guys. You're going to need help making sure little kids don't get off the trail, answering questions, and other stuff. Besides, I don't care if I win anything or not."

"Cool. Thanks, Colt. Melissa, I feel bad that you can't do it. Maybe you should start working for us after it's over."

"No way. For one thing, I need to start paying for Mocha's board, and I don't want to disappoint your mom. She said she needs the help now."

Tori sighed. "Then I'm with the rest of you. I'm not going to take part in the hunt alone. Where's the fun in that?"

Chapter Eight

Kate hung the sawdust fork on a hook, then pivoted toward her friends. "I don't know about you guys, but I think we need to do some sleuthing."

Melissa's brows rose. "I have no idea what you just said."

Tori grinned. "Yeah! Like Nancy Drew!"

Melissa crossed her arms. "Huh? Speak English."

Kate sank onto a bale of straw. "Seriously? You've never read The Nancy Drew Files or any of the old Nancy Drew books? My grandmother has all of the old ones, and my mom grew up reading the newer Nancy Drew Files. They're mysteries written for kids our age, and they're really good."

Colt grunted. "Like I'd read books for girls."

Melissa smirked. "See. I'm not the only one who didn't know what you're talking about. And I've never heard of sleuthing. What is it?"

"For the record," Colt interrupted, "I didn't say I didn't know. Just that I didn't read those books. I read the Hardy Boys mysteries. They're pretty old too, but my dad got me hooked on them 'cause I love a good mystery. Kate, explain what you're talking about."

"A sleuth is someone who follows clues, so we need to talk about everything we know about the theft, or think we know, make some deductions, and plan a course of action to follow the clues the thief might have left behind. That's what Nancy and her friends always did. They snooped around, figured out clues, and followed them until they discovered what happened."

Tori smiled. "Yeah, but sometimes they got into trouble or danger doing it. So we don't want to copy them too much."

Melissa gave a slow nod. "Okay. I get it. But do we have any clues?"

Tori bounced a little on the adjoining bale, her warm brown eyes sparkling. "Sure we do. Mr. Wallace complained about the noise and the traffic. He totally changed his tune when he saw Mrs. Ferris's box."

"Yeah," Kate said. "In fact, he was really insistent we tell her he'd like to buy it."

"All right." Melissa uncrossed her arms and leaned against the wall behind the bale. "What else?"

Colt plucked at the bale of straw. "And remember, we met some other people who commented on the box or acted really interested. What were their names?"

"There were several. Like Mr. Creighton, who owns a business in town. His daughter is Molly," Kate explained.

Colt nodded. "Those college kids ... the one who eyed the box is Jerry Meyers. I know Jerry—or I should say, I know his younger brother, Jake. Nice kid, but Jerry has always been kind of wild."

"Oh, and Mr. Abbington," Tori added.

Kate turned to look Tori in the eye. "Yeah ... I told Mom she needed to keep the box in the house after he came."

"Kate ..." Melissa hesitated. "Do you know if the box was ever opened in front of the customers? Did your mom put money in it when people were in the office?"

"No way." Kate shook her head, and her braid swung across her shoulder. "She said she didn't want anyone to know that's where she was keeping the money. And she always locked the box and put the key in her pocket before she left the office. She never kept it in the barn until we used it to store the entry fees. That's why she was so surprised it was taken. How would the thief know it held all the money?"

Colt shrugged. "Maybe he didn't. In fact, he still might not know."

"Huh?" Kate, Tori, and Melissa chorused.

"Think about it. It's old and could be valuable. And based on what at least two people said, it probably is. Maybe the thief didn't know he was taking the money. He simply loved the box. Although I do remember one time you mentioned we were keeping the money in it, Kate."

Kate's eyes widened. "Yikes!" She slapped her forehead. "I can't believe I did that. But you have a good point. It might be someone who wanted the box because it's old or pretty. Like Mr. Wallace, who wanted to buy it."

"Exactly. Now we have to figure out which one of them took it."

Tori slumped. "*If* any of them did. It could be someone else entirely. I don't see how we can find out."

Kate didn't want to hurt Tori's feelings, but she wished her friend wouldn't give up so easily.

Then Tori held up her hand. "Hold it! I've got it! I know the perfect way to find out if it's in Mr. Wallace's house." She gave another bounce on the hay, her face beaming.

Relief hit Kate, along with guilt for not giving Tori a chance to think and come up with an idea. After all, hadn't Kate herself doubted God not long ago? "So spill, Tori."

Tori giggled. "Right. Sorry. Remember how we baked cookies and took them to Mrs. Maynard to apologize for trespassing on her property? I mean, how Kate and I baked them, then took them over?"

Melissa snorted. "And didn't tell me about it until it was over."

Tori shrugged. "Because you said you didn't want to go back. Anyway, why not do that with Mr. Wallace?"

Colt wrinkled his nose. "How's that gonna help?"

"Well, see, we take them over and tell him we're sorry for all the traffic and noise. Then we ask him if he still wants to buy Mrs. Ferris's antique box. If he says yes, we know he's not the one."

Kate gave a slow nod. "But if he says no …"

Melissa squealed and hugged Tori. "You're brilliant! If he says no, then we've got him! He's our thief!"

"Not so fast." Colt held up his hand. "Even if he is the thief, how do we prove it? It's not like we can hand him the cookies, ask him a question, then accuse him right there on his porch. And what if he says yes? It's not like your mom would sell the box even if she had it."

"Hmm, good point," Kate admitted. "I guess we need to think this through."

Color rose in Melissa's cheeks. "Now I feel really silly for getting all excited. But there's got to be a way to find out."

"There is," Colt said. "If he says he still wants to buy it, but he read the article saying it was stolen, we'll tell him we'll pass the word to Kate's mom in case it's returned. That will give him a chance to turn it in if he's feeling guilty. It's not like we're promising he can buy it. If he says he's not interested, we get inside his house somehow and find that box."

Tori looked nervous. "That's breaking and entering."

"Not if he invites us in." Colt grinned. "We can tell him we're really thirsty from the hot weather and ask if he'd let us come in to have a drink of water. Then maybe one of you girls could ask to use the bathroom while we keep him busy. You could peek in a couple of rooms while we get water in the kitchen and talk to Mr. Wallace."

"Okay …" Kate said the word, but she wasn't sure if she totally agreed. "But what if we get caught? How about you do the snooping, Colt, and the three of us will keep him occupied?"

"Sure, I can do that. I've read enough mysteries to know you have to be sneaky and keep quiet. And if he catches me, I'll apologize for opening the wrong door. If he's the thief, this is the only way we'll ever find out. It's not like he's going to come forward and offer to return a box full of money he stole."

Tori scrunched her brows. "If he saw the article appealing to the thief, he might be too embarrassed to return it, since he's a neighbor and all."

"I agree," Kate said. "I don't think he'll return it either. Sounds like a good plan to me, if Colt's willing to do the searching. How about you guys?"

Melissa and Tori nodded. Then Melissa shot Tori an encouraging look. "I think the idea was brilliant—asking if Mr. Wallace wants to buy the box—but I'm not crazy about snooping in his house." She slapped her hands on her thighs. "I guess we just hope we don't get caught, or it's gonna be totally embarrassing for us, not him, since we don't have any proof he's the thief."

Colt jumped up from the bale of straw. "Then let's go catch us a thief!"

Kate gaped at him. "Now?"

"Why not? You girls start baking, and I'll plan my strategy on what I'll do once we get inside."

Kate eyed him, still not certain about the plan. But it was the best they had, and the only hope of getting the money back. She clenched her hands into fists. They had to make it work. It wasn't fair that Pete and other deserving kids might not get to go to camp because of one selfish person.

"All right. Let's do it." She pivoted, then marched up the alleyway toward the house, determined to catch the thief.

A picture of Mr. Wallace kicking them out of his house and calling their parents flashed into her mind, but she pushed it away. Failure was *not* an option.

Chapter Nine

It didn't take long to mix up and bake a batch of snickerdoodles. A couple of hours later, Kate and her three friends stood on the doorstep of Mr. Wallace's house, cookies in hand.

Kate couldn't stop her knees from shaking. It was a good thing Melissa was carrying the plate of cookies and planned on talking. At least *her* hands were steady.

Colt knocked on the door, and Tori leaned close to whisper in Kate's ear. "I sure hope this turns out okay. I'm nervous."

Kate nodded, but she didn't speak as the door swung open.

Mr. Wallace gave a start, then peered closer at the kids through his thick glasses. "What can I do for you young folks?" He ran a hand over his iron-gray hair and glanced back into the house.

Kate stiffened. Was he already feeling guilty or maybe even trapped? Did he guess why they were there, and was he trying to plan a way to escape? A loud noise carried from inside the house.

How silly—the TV is on, and he's probably upset we interrupted whatever he's watching.

Melissa extended the plate. "Hello, Mr. Wallace. Kate—I mean we—thought we'd bring you a batch of fresh-baked snicker-doodles." She gave him a sweet smile.

"What for?" He glanced over his shoulder again.

"Uh ... to say we're sorry for all the bother recently."

"What's that?" He turned his entire attention on Melissa now. "What bother? Have you been over here bothering me when I didn't know it?"

"No, of course not." She seemed a little flustered now and definitely nervous. She licked her lips and held out the plate again. "Would you care for some cookies? They're still warm."

"But what are they for?" He kept a firm grip on the edge of the door, not opening it any more than the width of his frame.

Kate could see Colt almost standing on tiptoe trying to peer inside, and she nudged him. They didn't want Mr. Wallace to suspect anything.

Melissa widened her smile. "You know. All those days when people were coming to the barn to sign up for the scavenger hunt—our trail ride. You came over and mentioned the traffic was annoying, so we wanted to apologize."

"Ah ... I see. Well, I suppose I could take them. Thank you." He reached out a hand, but she took a half step back.

Kate moved up beside her. "We had one other thing you might be interested in. We wondered if you'd still like to purchase that antique box you noticed in the office that belongs to my mom."

"What's that? A box? I don't remember a box."

Kate's heartbeat intensified, and she shot a glance at Melissa. She gave a nod that could barely be seen, and Kate looked at Mr. Wallace again. "You know—the old antique box. You told me to let you know if she ever decided to sell it."

He reached for the plate of cookies. "Don't remember a box. Thanks for the cookies."

Colt touched the man's arm. "It's such a hot day. We were in a hurry to get here, and we didn't bring our water bottles." He chuckled. "We didn't even take time to eat any cookies ourselves. Would you mind if we come in and get a drink of water?"

Mr. Wallace eyed them, then peered over his shoulder again. Finally he sighed. "I suppose. Come along." He grabbed the plate, then hurried down the short hall, with all four of them following.

He stopped in the kitchen and waved toward the sink. "Glasses are to the right in the cupboard, but I'm not sure if there's any clean ones. You might try the dishwasher. I have coffee on. I don't suppose any of you drink that at your age?"

Tori shook her head and opened her mouth, but nothing came out.

Colt smiled. "I don't, but thanks. Maybe the girls can wash a coffee cup for you and glasses for the rest of us, if you don't mind?"

He lifted a shoulder. "Suit yourself. There's plenty of dirty ones in the sink."

Kate's nose tingled with disgust. The place stunk. The sink was stacked with dishes that appeared to have been there for days. Crumbs and something sticky dotted the surface to the right of the sink, and the worn linoleum floor squeaked as she took another step. A fly flew past her nose and landed on the rim of a glass. She felt as if she was going to hurl.

Colt cleared his throat. She looked at him, and he waggled his eyebrows, then pivoted and faced Mr. Wallace. "Would you mind if I use your bathroom while the girls visit with you and wash your dishes?"

Tori gave a soft moan. "Dishes?" She mouthed the word.

Melissa grabbed a handle next to the faucet and flipped on the hot water. "Yeah, come on, Tori. You and I will start. Kate, why don't you take the plastic off the cookies and see that Mr. Wallace helps himself while Colt finds the bathroom?"

Colt disappeared in a different direction than they'd come.

Kate watched him go with a lump in her throat. *Please don't get caught. Please don't get caught.* The words repeated themselves over and over in her mind without stopping. She leaned over the plate that Mr. Wallace had set in the middle of the cluttered kitchen table. "So, Mr. Wallace, have you had snickerdoodles before?" It was a lame thing to say, but she couldn't think of anything else at the moment. If she wasn't careful, she'd be saying "Please don't get caught" aloud, which wouldn't do at all.

Mr. Wallace inhaled three cookies while Tori and Melissa washed a few glasses and a mug. Kate grabbed a towel and dried them, then poured the coffee. "Do you take it black?" Thankfully her voice didn't squeak.

"Yes." He extended a hand while he reached for another cookie with the other. "These are good, thank you. But you kids had better get your drinks and head home. I'm sure your parents are wondering what's taking so long. Don't want you to get in trouble." He took a sip and set the mug down. "Now where's that boy? He's taking an awfully long time to use the bathroom."

Kate nearly jumped in front of him when he rose. "Wouldn't you like another cookie to go with that coffee?"

He shook his head. "No. I'm going to check on that boy. What did you say his name is?"

"Co-co-colt." Kate pressed her lips together and aimed a panicked glance at Melissa and Tori. "Now what?" she mouthed.

Tori's round eyes stared back at her, and Melissa didn't speak. Suddenly a loud crash echoed from down the hall, and Mr. Wallace bolted from the room with a roar.

Chapter Ten

Tori swung toward Kate. "What should we do? Will he hurt Colt?" Her normally dusky face looked as pale as Melissa's.

Melissa glanced from Kate to Tori. "We'd better find out. But be ready to make a run for the front door if we have to."

Kate raced for the doorway where Colt had disappeared what seemed aeons ago. "If Colt isn't hurt and can run. That crash sounded bad." She dashed down a short hall past stacks of papers, trying to figure out where to go next. Three doors opened off the hall, but an open archway ahead beckoned.

A moan emanated from the room. Kate skidded to a stop in the doorway and blinked, not sure what she was seeing. Stacks of newspapers and magazines as high as her shoulders lined the wall in rows. A wide spot in the middle of the room contained an easy chair and a TV, along with a side table next to the chair covered with more dirty dishes and a dust-covered lamp. "Colt? Where are you? Mr. Wallace? What happened?"

"I'm over here." Colt's voice came from the far side of the room, and Kate suddenly noticed Mr. Wallace bending over a pile of magazines and newspapers. She and the girls rushed forward.

Kate stopped, then leaned over what she could see of Colt. His head, shoulders, and chest were free, and Mr. Wallace was carefully moving more clumps of papers from around Colt's waist. Kate shook her head, trying to clear it of the fear that had gripped her the past minute or so. "Are you hurt? Can you get up?'"

Mr. Wallace glowered at Colt. "You messed up my row. I had it all organized and neat, and you messed it up. You need to go home now." He raised his head and growled. "All of you."

Colt rolled out from under the last of the magazines and tried to stand but lost his balance on a wobbly stack of papers under his foot. He flailed his arms and pitched forward toward another row. Kate and Tori jumped forward and grabbed his arms, pulling him back before he sent it tumbling as well.

Colt pressed his hands against the shivering mass of paper and moaned. "That was close. Why do you have all of these, Mr. Wallace? I'm sorry I knocked them over. I must have gotten turned around as to how to get back to the kitchen. Then I slipped on a glossy magazine that was on the floor, and the next thing I knew, all of this was coming down on top of me."

Tori shuddered. "This stuff is heavy. You could have been seriously hurt."

Mr. Wallace's red face dripped with perspiration. "Get your cookie plate and leave my house this instant. It's going to take me the rest of the day to get all of these stacked the way they were before." He wrung his hands. "Oh my, what will I do now? Such a disaster. All these beautiful magazines and precious papers damaged. Oh my." He turned his back on them and bent to pick up a stack.

Colt dusted off his jeans. "I'm really sorry, Mr. Wallace. Would you like us to stay and help you clean up? We can stack the magazines fast."

"No!" He swiveled and pointed toward the kitchen. "I'll do it myself. Just get your plate and go."

Kate led the way through the stacks of periodicals and papers, shaking her head. What would make a person collect all this stuff? If this place ever caught on fire … She shivered thinking about it.

The four of them slipped out the front door after retrieving Kate's plate. Colt shut the door carefully behind them. "That was pretty weird." He rubbed his shin. "I had no idea a stack of magazines could hurt so much. I'll probably have bruises on top of bruises tomorrow."

They walked down the gravel road, heading for home. Tori clutched the empty plate to her chest and stopped walking. "So … did you find anything?"

Melissa and Kate halted and stared at Colt.

He motioned with his hand. "Come on. Let's get out of earshot. Mr. Wallace might decide to slip out the back door and follow us to make sure we're gone."

They started up again, but Kate shook her head. "That man is too worried about his mess to care about us. What do they call people like that? I know there's a name for it."

"Hoarders," Melissa said. "Funny that it was only in his living room and hall. There weren't any piles in his kitchen."

Colt snorted. "That's about the only place that didn't have them. I opened two doors besides the bathroom. Every room had stacks of papers and magazines. It would take a lifetime to collect that many. I don't get it."

"It's a sickness," Tori explained. "I heard my mom and dad talking about a lady my mom knows. She won't let anyone come to her house because she's the same way. I don't remember what she collects, but her house is pretty full, according to Mom. It's really sad."

An instant later Melissa peeked over her shoulder. "We're a long way from Mr. Wallace's house, Colt. Did you see the box? And why did you take so long? We were getting worried. Then we heard that loud crash. Mr. Wallace bellowed like you'd broken his favorite treasure, and we figured you were done for. So tell us everything and don't leave a thing out!"

A dozen more strides brought them to the paddock area of the Blue Ribbon Barn, and they sank onto the grassy stretch and propped themselves against the wood rails. Colt plucked a blade of grass but only fiddled with it between his fingers. "When I left the kitchen, I headed down the hallway that leads from the kitchen to the living room. You probably noticed three doors along the hallway, right?"

They all nodded.

"Well, I could hear you girls clattering dishes and talking, and since Mr. Wallace is older, I figured his hearing might not be great, and it would be safe to open the first door, if I was super quiet. It was a bedroom." He grunted. "You could see a bed and dresser, but I don't think the box was there. Boxes of stuff were piled on the bed and stacked against the wall. I didn't even go in. Full boxes blocked the closet door, and there was no place for Mrs. Ferris's box to be, so I left and tried the next door."

Colt flicked the blade of grass away as if it annoyed him, then grabbed another one. "The next bedroom was his, but there was stuff in there too. But not as much, and the closet door was open. I tiptoed in and looked, but I've got to tell you, I felt terrible. It's not right to go into other people's bedrooms." He stared at his shoes. "I didn't touch anything, and I didn't see the box, so I left. The last room was the bathroom, and it's tiny. Nothing in there either. In fact, I'm surprised Mr. Wallace showed any interest in ever buying that box. He doesn't have a single item that indicates he's a collector of anything but junk."

"I wondered about that," Melissa said. "He might even have a trace of Alzheimer's … especially since he doesn't remember he wanted to buy the box—or that he even saw it."

Kate groaned. "That's awful! We made him let us into his house, snooped around, and then knocked over his stack of stuff."

Tori smiled. "But he loved the cookies. And there's a good chance that by tomorrow, he won't remember we came anyway. I'm just glad no one got hurt. He was more upset about his papers getting disturbed than anything else. But we apologized already, and I don't think we should go back."

"No chance." Kate shook her head. "I'm never going there again if I can help it. But I do feel bad we thought he was the thief. Instead he's a lonely old man whose main interest in life is collecting junk. I'm going to tell Mom about him, and maybe she can invite him to church or have him over to our house for supper sometime."

Melissa looked from one friend to the other. "You might be right that Mr. Wallace isn't the thief, but we'd better not rule him out. I mean, what's to say he wasn't faking? He could have Alzheimer's, but he also might have hidden the box and put on a great act." She shrugged. "But I could be wrong. So now what? Colt got all those bruises for nothing, and no box. What's the next clue we're going to follow? Whatever it is, I sure hope it's safer and cleaner than this last one!"

Chapter Eleven

The next morning, after completing chores at the barn, Kate stepped onto the mounting block next to Capri and grinned across her back at Tori, who stood beside Starlight. "It's so great to be riding again instead of only working on the scavenger hunt." She put her foot in the stirrup, then swung her leg over the saddle. "I'm so excited we get to take a jumping lesson at last."

Tori settled into her saddle and gathered her reins. "No jumping for me. I'm going to work on my posting and getting the correct lead on a canter. I'll stay on the outside of the ring while Mrs. Jamison takes you through your paces on the inside of the arena." She smiled at Melissa, who was sitting patiently on Mocha, then waved at Colt, who leaned against the rail on the outside of the arena. "Hey, Melissa. Isn't this going to be boring for you?"

Melissa shook her head. "It never hurts a horse to go back to the beginning and have a refresher. Besides, I can't turn down a free lesson, can I? It was sure nice of Mrs. Jamison to include me today." She stroked Mocha's neck. "Colt's the one who's going to get bored. Why aren't you riding?"

He grinned. "Lazy, I guess. I've been riding a lot lately, and I'm tired of arena work. When you finish here, we should head out on the trail we're going to use for the scavenger hunt and scope out some places to hide items."

Kate groaned. "Now you've made me want to go do that instead of taking a lesson." She slapped her hand over her mouth, then removed it quickly. "Nope. I never said that. I've been waiting too long to do more than trot over cavaletti poles and twelve-inch jumps. But I *am* looking forward to checking out the course we'll take for the trail ride. Great idea, Colt."

He arched a brow. "Told you boys are smart."

She rolled her eyes. "Whatever."

Mrs. Jamison entered the far end of the arena and glanced at the girls. "Ready to go? Tori, you're staying on the outside of the ring and working on basic skills, right?"

"Yes, ma'am. Sure am. Kate and Melissa can have the jumping all to themselves."

"All right. Let's warm up your horses, then. Go around the outer edge of the arena at a walk, then two more times at a trot. Think about your posture, your hands, and your leg position, and post at the trot. Now begin."

For the next few minutes, Kate and her friends concentrated on warming up their horses while working on their equitation. It was so fun to be taking a lesson with Tori and Melissa! Kate no longer felt envy when she watched Melissa ride as she had at first. Now she was simply content that Mocha was well and Melissa was their friend and able to ride her own horse once again.

"Tori, I want you to keep posting and keep constant contact with Starlight's mouth. Every two circles, reverse direction so you can post on the other diagonal."

Tori nodded and reversed direction. "Could you remind me what that means? It's been a while since I heard it explained."

Mrs. Jamison tapped her crop against her breeches. "Certainly. Keep your reins just tight enough so you can feel the movement of your horse's head through the reins. If it's too tight, your horse will toss his head. If it's too loose and you can't feel any contact, then Starlight might decide to do whatever he wants to and ignore your instructions. Does that make sense?"

"Yes, thanks." Tori reversed direction again.

"Kate and Melissa, come to the center." Both girls moved toward their instructor. "I've got the jumps set at only eighteen inches to start. Then we'll go to twenty-four. I know that's not much for Mocha or Capri, but I want to work on form today rather than height. We want to be sure you girls understand the correct pacing between the jumps at a trot and a canter, while remembering your position in the saddle and keeping contact with your horse's mouth. Melissa, will you begin? Take the poles at a walk first, then circle around and take them at a trot, then a canter."

Kate let her breath out in a soft whoosh, thankful Mrs. Jamison hadn't asked her to go first. She'd done a lot of walk, trot, and canter exercises over rails a foot off the ground, but she'd never cantered over jumps or gone higher than twelve inches. This was going to be fun—but she hoped she didn't mess up. Capri knew what she was doing, and the last thing Kate wanted was to undo any of her training by doing something stupid.

Mocha trotted with a smooth, fluid stride, acting as though the low jumps didn't even exist. Melissa leaned forward slightly in her saddle, each hand holding a rein, and the heels of her hands placed a few inches ahead of Mocha's withers but not planted so firmly her arms stayed rigid. Kate needed to remember that—not to grip the reins so tightly that she'd jar Capri's mouth when her mare stretched a little to go over a jump. She had to flow with her horse and allow her arms to extend and her hands to soften when Capri needed a bit more rein. There was so much to think about all at once.

Melissa and Mocha took the final jump at a canter, making it look as though they were one unit rather than a girl perched on a horse.

Mrs. Jamison smiled. "Nicely done, Melissa. Kate, I want you to take Capri through at a trot first. Then we'll see if you feel comfortable cantering. You've done well at cavalettis and twelve-inch jumps, so you shouldn't have trouble with this. Go when you're ready."

Kate gathered her reins and barely squeezed with her calves. Capri responded immediately, as if she was anxious for her turn. Kate was grateful Mrs. Jamison was starting them out low and slow. Kate took the first pass at a walk with no problem, and it helped her relax. She concentrated on not having a death grip on the reins and on keeping her heels down and her focus forward as she'd been taught.

"Good job. Now let's go through again at a trot—twice. That will allow you to think about posting and the pacing between the jumps. No rushing. Keep your horse's stride even. Good. That's right."

Mrs. Jamison's voice followed Kate over each bar, helping her focus on what she was doing instead of thinking about her nerves. She could do this! Sure, there was a lot to think about at once, but the more she did it, the more natural it felt.

Mrs. Jamison held up her hand. "Once more. Think about your hand position this time. You're bumping Capri's mouth every time she goes over the bar."

Kate loosened her tight grip on the reins but still kept a firm hold on the leather. She pulled to a stop after clearing the last bar. "That felt better. Was it okay?"

"Yes. Much better that time. How do you feel about trying the bars at a canter?"

"I'm nervous, but I want to do it."

"Great." She swung around. "Tori, go ahead and walk Starlight for the next three or four rounds. He's been trotting for quite a while now, so let's give him a rest. I want you to think about keeping your heels down, your spine straight, your chin up, and your hands steady as you walk."

Tori nodded and pulled Starlight into a walk.

"All right now, Kate. Do a circle around the arena at a canter, staying inside of Tori's track, and when you're ready, head down the center and put Capri over the rails. You'll want a little more contact with your reins but still keep your arms and hands fluid. And don't forget to lean forward the slightest bit before she takes the jump. Got that?"

Kate's mind whirled. "I think so. How about keeping her on the correct lead around the arena? Does that matter for now?"

"Yes, it always matters. When you straighten her and point her toward the rails, start thinking about the other things I told you. Go when you're ready."

Melissa gave her an encouraging smile. "You can do it, Kate. Relax and have fun."

Kate exhaled. That was exactly what she needed to hear. "Thanks, Melissa." She tipped Capri's head slightly to the outside of the circle and bumped her with her inside heel, asking for a canter. Her mare instantly moved forward on the correct lead, her outside leg extending farther than the inside, while staying in a short, collected, but smooth canter.

"Good job on that lead!" Mrs. Jamison's voice carried across the arena. "Whenever you're ready, come to the center and take the first rail."

Kate's heart pounded almost in time with Capri's hoofbeats as they neared the first rail. She remembered too late to slow Capri, and her mare's front hooves scraped the pole. Kate reined Capri in to keep her from rushing, and they popped over the second rail without any trouble. By the third and fourth, Kate was beginning to feel as though she had the pacing down a little better, but she had no clue if she'd leaned forward when she was supposed to or kept her hands and arms fluid enough. It all happened so quickly, and her entire focus had been on not knocking down one of the low rails. She pulled to a stop several yards from Mrs. Jamison.

Her instructor smiled. "How do you think you did?"

Kate detailed what she'd been thinking and ended with, "There's a lot to remember in a short amount of time. All I could think about was getting the pacing right and keeping Capri from rushing. I think she was excited to be jumping again."

Mrs. Jamison nodded. "Exactly. But as soon as you asked her to slow and reminded her to put her mind on her job, she did. There *is* a lot to remember, which is why jumping is a discipline and requires hours of practice. Don't worry. It will come in time, and we'll work on the things you're struggling with. But you did well for your first time. I'm going to have you go through your paces again, taking two more rounds; then we'll raise the bar to two and a half feet for Melissa. I'd like you to stay at this level for this lesson, Kate, and we'll consider raising the bar for your next lesson, if you practice between now and next week."

"Okay." Kate wasn't sure how she felt. Disappointed … relieved … a bit embarrassed in front of Melissa, who got to move on. But she knew that was silly. Melissa had been jumping for years, and Kate had barely started. She sat up straighter in her saddle. "I'll try to think about as much as I can this time through, and I'll watch Melissa. She's good, and I know I can learn from what she does."

She turned to Melissa in time to see a pinched expression fade and a smile take its place.

Mrs. Jamison waved toward Melissa. "Go ahead and trot your horse ahead of Tori as Kate takes her next round. Keep Mocha warmed up."

Kate took her final turn, then joined Tori and Melissa at trotting around the arena while Mrs. Jamison raised the level of the rails.

Melissa pulled alongside her. "Nice job on that last round. Your pacing was excellent, and your posture was great."

Joy blossomed in Kate's heart. She kept Capri to the inside of Mocha and at the same pace. "Seriously? Cool! It's all so new and confusing."

"You're a natural. If you keep practicing, it won't be long until you're clearing the three-foot rails and higher."

Kate smiled, trying to remember why she'd ever disliked this girl. "Thanks. You're coming with us on the trail ride to check out places to hide the clues after we're done, right?"

Melissa brightened. "Sure! Can't wait to get outside and onto a trail with friends. Looks like Mrs. Jamison is ready." She lifted a hand. "Wish me luck."

Kate's smile widened to a grin. "You don't need it. You're a pro."

Chapter Twelve

Colt was saddled and waiting outside when the girls finished their lesson. Kate stroked Capri's neck as she rode her mare out the large double doors at the end of the arena. Tori followed on Starlight, with Melissa right behind. Kate turned in her saddle as soon as they reached Colt. "Did you see how great Melissa did on that last round of jumps?"

He swung up onto Romeo's back. "Nope. I was busy getting ready to go."

Melissa waved a hand. "It's Mocha that did great. I just sat there."

Kate's braid swished against her neck. "No way can you get away with saying that now. It's way harder than it looks."

Tori giggled. "I could have told you that a long time ago. I've always thought it looked hard. I'm very happy riding English pleasure and equitation—that's enough for me. But you're right, Kate. Melissa did great, and so did you."

Colt bumped his horse with his heel. "Now that we've got that settled, let's hit the trail. I'm about jumped out. Give me wide open spaces or woods any day."

Kate urged Capri forward to catch him. "I've only ridden this trail once with Mom. Are you familiar with it?"

"Yep. It's nice that you can go up the road for only a quarter of a mile before you hit state land. One of the neighbors gave permission to ride through their open fields as part of the hunt. It will make it more interesting that way, and we can make a giant circle and end up back where we started."

"Right." Kate looked over her shoulder at Tori and Melissa talking and smiling. It didn't give her the pang of jealousy it once had, and she was glad. She'd learned that jealousy and envy were ugly emotions and did nothing to make her a better person. Besides, Melissa had turned out to be much nicer than they'd ever dreamed, and she was actually fun to have around. "Hey, you guys! We need to go single file for the next few hundred yards. Then we'll hit a trail. Colt's going to lead the way. Keep your eyes open for good hiding spots for the clues."

Melissa raised her voice. "Speaking of clues, we need to talk about what we're going to do next to find that missing box. We can't let that go and lose all the money we raised."

"I agree." Kate slowed Capri and fell in behind Colt, just ahead of Melissa. "Have you and Tori come up with any ideas?"

"We might have." Melissa waited until a car passed before she continued. "Sure glad most people around here know to slow down for horses on the road. Not all horses are as calm as ours about traffic."

"No kidding," Tori said. "I'd never even try this if I wasn't riding Starlight. He's the best."

Kate could hear the pride in her friend's voice, and joy filled her heart. How cool that Tori finally had her own horse, and the four of them could go riding together! "So what did you guys come up with, Tori?"

"Melissa can tell you. Colt won't be able to hear if I try. I don't talk loud enough."

Colt turned onto the trail, sparsely populated with tall firs that dotted a meadow. "There's a good trail through most of this. I heard that other people use it for horseback riding and bicycles. There's no motorized traffic allowed on it. We might meet someone riding a bike or jogging, so keep a firm hold on your reins in case your horse spooks." He glanced back. "Everybody good?"

"Yep," a chorus of voices answered.

Melissa picked up where Tori left off. "We should go to the store Mr. Creighton owns and chat. We can snoop around a little. If he took the box, it might be in his office."

Kate reined Capri around a stump on the edge of the trail. "Hey, Colt. There's a hollow spot under the roots of this stump. We could hide something there, right?"

He pulled to a stop. "Sure. Does it look deep enough to put small objects in?"

She peered down. "I think so. It's pretty dark in there. And we could write a clue about an ancient giant with hollow toes."

Melissa laughed as she stopped Mocha beside Capri. "I love that! It will make the scavenger hunters think and keep their eyes open. But you know, we'll need to send people different routes so they aren't riding on top of each other. And at least a couple of the items will need to be hidden in or around the barn, and some will be on your property as well. Otherwise, we'll have everyone following everyone else on the trail and seeing who finds what. That won't be fun at all."

Kate considered the idea. "That makes sense. I think we're going to need to put a little more thought into how we do this, but I like your suggestion. This is all new to me. Colt, what do you think about going to Mr. Creighton's business?"

"There's no way he'd leave that box out where anyone can see it. I think his office makes more sense than keeping it at his house. His wife or daughter could stumble across it there. It's more apt to stay hidden in his office. Not sure how we'd get in, though, without him accusing us of trying to rob him or something. We'll need to give it more thought."

"Maybe we could sneak in there at night with flashlights," Melissa suggested.

Kate shook her head. "Someone would see us and call the police. Besides, that's breaking and entering, and our parents would notice if we were gone at night."

"My mom wouldn't," Melissa whispered.

Silence fell over them as they took in her words.

A minute later, Colt cleared his throat. "I had another idea too. But not about Mr. Creighton."

All three girls pinned their attention on Colt. "Remember I told you I know Jerry's younger brother, Jake? Jerry Meyers is the college kid we were wondering about. I don't think he'd know an antique from a piece of junk, but if he knew the cash was stored in it … well, it's possible he took it."

Capri danced a couple of steps as if anxious to get moving, and Kate stroked her neck. "Easy, girl. We'll go soon. I'd think you'd be tired after jumping." She looked up. "So how does knowing Jake help us?"

"I'm not sure. Maybe we could go visit him sometime— or have him over to the barn. You know, see if his brother has brought anything new home lately. Jake isn't a big fan of Jerry's, and Jerry has teased Jake and been mean to him most of his life. I'm guessing Jake would be happy to help us if he knew."

"Cool." Kate looked at the rest of them. "What do you think?"

Melissa narrowed her eyes. "I'm not sure. I know what it's like to have someone hang out with you because they want something from you. I'm not sure it's right to do that to Jake. I mean, he's not one of your regular friends is he, Colt?"

"Naw. He's a little younger than me, and his mom home-schools him, so I see him at homeschool functions, but we've never been close. But he's a good kid—not *too* annoying. He's not into horses, but he's crazy about movies and dogs. He's try-ing to train an older puppy they got. Melissa, you and Kate both have dogs—maybe we could offer to give him some pointers. It's not like we have to invite him over, then send him home as soon as we find out what he knows. We can hang out with him for a while and help with his dog if you want. What do you think, Melissa? Sound okay to you?"

"Yeah, I guess. I just don't want him to feel used like I have in the past." She held up her hand. "Not by you guys; I don't mean that. And we'd better finish this ride. Mocha is getting edgy from standing so long."

They headed down the trail, agreeing to keep their eyes open for more good spots to hide clues, as well as thinking about ways to find the stolen box. But Kate couldn't think about anything but Melissa's expression when she talked about her friends using her to get what they wanted. Kate almost shuddered at the memory of how she and her friends treated Melissa when they first met. To be fair, Melissa had had a chip on her shoulder and wasn't a nice person to be around, but that didn't excuse Kate for her actions or attitude.

One thing she'd keep in mind from now on when she met someone new: You couldn't possibly know what made a person act the way she did if you didn't know anything about her past or what her life was like at home. Melissa's dad had left them almost broke, sending her mom into a spiral of drinking and sleeping to hide from the pain. From the way Melissa talked sometimes, she practically didn't have parents.

What was this Jake like, whose brother had been mean to him all his life? Would he be a beaten-down person who was always negative and not fun to be around? Did that even matter? She couldn't shake what Melissa had said. There was no way they wanted to make Jake feel used—to get information from him and then dump him. But they had to find that stolen box, and Jake might hold the key to doing so if his older brother Jerry had it. She wasn't crazy about adding anyone else to their circle of friends—it was so comfortable now that Melissa finally fit in. But it didn't mean the kid would want to stick around either. Why did something new always have to come up to change things?

Chapter Thirteen

A couple of hours later, Colt hung up the phone in Kate's house and grinned. "Jake said he can bring his puppy over now, if we're willing to help him. I guess it's not really a puppy. They got him at six months old, and they've had him for two months. His parents told Jake if he can't learn to control the dog, they'll find it a new home, so he was pretty excited about getting help."

Kate rested her back against the refrigerator door. "We need to remember what Melissa said. Jake can bring his dog over again after today if he wants to, even if he doesn't know anything about Jerry."

Melissa smiled. "Good plan, Kate. I don't know if you remember me telling Pete early this summer that I got a puppy. He's eight months old now, and I've been doing obedience work with him." She hesitated. "Before my dad left, he helped me train Rex. Kate, you've done work with Rufus too, right?"

Kate nodded. "Yes. He'll sit and stay when I tell him to, but I've been busy lately, so I haven't worked with him as much as I should. This will be a good refresher for him too. It's a great idea!"

Colt gestured behind Kate. "Got anything cold in there to drink, or are you blocking the door to keep us out?" He patted his stomach. "I'm getting pretty thin with all this riding and thinking, so I could use a few extra calories. Maybe even a cookie if you have any left from the batch you baked for Mr. Wallace."

Thirty minutes later a car door slammed outside, then a knock sounded on the door. Kate opened it and saw a slim, wiry boy with straight brown hair, who stood a good six inches shorter than her, wearing horn-rimmed glasses and holding the leash on a half-grown Saint Bernard.

"Wow!" She stared at the dog. "He's going to be as big as Lulu when he's done growing!"

The boy's mouth twisted in a grin, and braces appeared. "Who's Lulu?" He cocked his head to the side. "That wouldn't happen to be a reference to 'Lulu' Louise Brooks, the actress from the 1920s and '30s who helped make the bobbed haircut famous? Because if so, she was considerably taller than Mouse will be."

"Mouse?" Nothing else would come out of Kate's mouth. All she could do was gape at this strange boy who pulled little-known facts from the air like magic.

Colt stepped next to Kate. "Hiya, Jake. This is Kate. Maybe I forgot to mention that Jake is a lover of all things movie and TV."

"Uh … yeah. I caught that. Want to come in?"

"Not yet. I need to tell my dad how long until he's supposed to pick me up again." He pushed his oversize glasses up to the bridge of his nose. "If you know, that is. Of course, I realize time is relative, and it's not something we can always be sure of. Kind of like in *Back to the Future*. Marty McFly had no idea his life would change in the time it took for a DeLorean to make an eighty-mile-an-hour jump into the future. But I don't suppose we're going back in time, or forward either, so we should be safe, right?"

Colt stifled a chuckle. "Yeah, I think it's safe to say we'll be sticking around here, Jake. Why don't you tell your dad an hour, and we'll see how it goes. It only takes him about five minutes to drive here, right?"

"Affirmative. That's what they say in—"

Colt held up his hand. "You'd better go talk to your dad, Jake. Let him know you'll call him if it ends up being longer."

"Right. Gotcha. Okay." He handed the leash to Kate, then spun around and tromped down the stairs and out to the car.

Kate held the leash up and stared at Colt, then at a gaping Tori and Melissa. "Is this kid for real?"

Colt's lips quirked. "Sorry I didn't warn you. But he's a good kid. Remember I said he wasn't *too* annoying?"

Tori snorted a laugh. "I think he's great! I mean, who knows all that stuff about movies and TV shows?"

Melissa took a step toward the dog. "And who calls a Saint Bernard 'Mouse,' and why?"

Jake bounded back up the steps, skipping the last one, and landed just inside the door. "Mouse is terrified of mice. So, the logic is, call him what he's afraid of, and eventually he'll get over it. Did you ever see the old movie *Of Mice and Men*? Not that it was really about mice, but the title is great, don't you think?" He retrieved the leash from Kate and blinked a couple of times behind his thick lenses.

Kate moistened her lips. "Uh-huh. That makes perfect sense. I think. Um … maybe we'd better take Mouse outside. I'm not sure Mom would be too happy about him being in the house."

"Agreed. Did you ever see the old Disney movie *Snowball Express*? It has a big Saint Bernard in it—Stoutheart. They let him stay in the house, but it was a huge ski lodge. He did break a thing or two and jumped on the bed in the middle of the night and broke it, because he was afraid. Just because dogs are big doesn't make them brave, you know." He cocked his head. "Maybe I should have named Mouse 'Stoutheart.' Do you suppose if I changed his name, it would make him braver?"

Kate stepped around him and out the door, but she couldn't contain a giggle. Tori was right. This kid was funny. "I think it would probably only confuse him. Besides, Mouse is gray and white. Mice are gray, so the name fits him, don't you think?"

The boy followed her, tugging at his dog. "Come on, Mouse. There's nothing to be afraid of. Yes, his color is very rare. Very few Saint Bernards are gray. Did you know a Saint Bernard is never a solid color? Not if it's a true Saint Bernard. There was another movie—"

Kate increased her pace, leaving her friends to appreciate the recitation of the movie facts. She'd planned to work with the dog in the barn, but he'd probably terrify the horses. The outdoor arena would definitely be better.

She rounded the corner and almost ran into Pete. "Hey, buddy, what's going on?"

The little boy was sitting on the grass next to his wading pool. He loved dipping his pail into the water and pouring it out, time after time. Something about the sound of the splashing water soothed him. Her mom sat nearby, reading a book in the shade.

"Hi, Mom."

Her mother looked up. "Hi, sweetie. What are you kids up to? Mrs. Jamison said you did really well with your lesson. You know we'll need to start cleaning stalls and feeding the horses in a couple of hours."

"Yeah, I know. We're going to help Jake Meyers with his dog."

She set her book down. "And who is Jake Meyers?"

Kate waved behind her as Colt led Jake, Mouse, and the girls toward them. "That's Jake and his dog, Mouse. Jake is home-schooled like Colt, and Colt knows Jake."

"Oh. I see. Mouse, is it? What an unusual name."

"Mom." Kate dropped her voice to a whisper. "I need to warn you. Don't ask Jake any questions. Just say hi and let him walk on by, okay? I'll explain later."

"Why ever not?" Her mother frowned, then turned her attention on Jake.

The boy stopped at the pool, and Mouse took a tentative step toward Pete.

The little boy squealed and opened his arms wide. "My friend!" He pushed to his knees and wrapped his arms around the dog's neck, burying his face in his fur.

Kate's mouth dropped open, and her mother looked as dazed as Kate felt.

Her mom tilted her head in wonder. "I'll be. He doesn't even treat Rufus like that." She sat upright, and fear crossed her features. "Rufus. Where is he? There's no one riding in the barn, so he's loose!"

Kate jumped as if she'd been kicked by a wild horse. "No way, Mom! He doesn't like other dogs. He'll get in a fight with

Mouse. Colt, help Jake hold Mouse's leash and get him away from Pete! Rufus is loose, and he's apt to attack Mouse!"

Her mother bolted from the lawn chair and scanned both directions. "Spread out, everybody. We've got to find Rufus. Don't call him. We don't want him to come to us with Pete here. He might get hurt if the dogs start fighting. Colt, would you stay with Pete and pick him up if you have to?"

"Sure, Mrs. Ferris. But Pete doesn't like me to touch him, and so he'll never let me hold him."

"I don't care what he wants right now. If Rufus comes this way, you grab Pete and head to the house."

She waited a second to make sure Colt understood, then waved her arms. "Spread out, everybody. Find that dog!"

Chapter Fourteen

Kate's heart beat like a three-hundred-pound drummer throwing his weight into his sticks as she raced toward the barn, praying she'd find Rufus before her dog discovered Mouse in his territory. How stupid could she get? Rufus was her dog and her responsibility—well, technically, he belonged to the entire family, but she'd done the most work with him. He was normally a sweet dog, but he could get aggressive if he thought another canine was invading his space.

"Rufus, come on, boy. Want to take a walk or go play?" She felt terrible promising something she wouldn't follow through with, since Rufus loved walks and knew exactly what she meant when she said it. She'd have to take him out later after her barn chores were finished. But that didn't matter now. She entered the quiet barn and whistled. "Rufus? Here, boy!" A horse nickered farther down the alleyway, but no dog barked or rushed out to greet her.

Tori and Melissa could be heard on the far side of the barn, calling Rufus and whistling. Her mom's strained voice came from outside, somewhere in the neighborhood of the outdoor arena where they'd been headed. Still no sound of her dog's answering bark.

She jogged through the barn, even opening the office and tack-room doors, since Rufus liked to sleep on the cool floors when it was too hot outside. She wondered if anyone had thought to check in the house. But no, he would have scented Mouse and rushed him as soon as they opened the door.

Suddenly Colt's whistle and loud shout came from where they'd left him with Pete, Jake, and Mouse. She clenched her hands and ran, praying the whole way she wouldn't arrive to a find a dogfight starting. "Please, God. Don't let Rufus or Mouse or Pete or anyone get hurt. Please, God, protect everyone."

She rounded the corner and almost collided with her mother, who'd skidded to a stop just a stride ahead. Kate grabbed her mom's arm to keep from knocking her over or falling herself. Her breath came in pants. "What's going on? Where's Rufus?"

Mom pointed, one hand shaking and the other covering her mouth. "Oh my. I never thought I'd see the day."

Kate stared where she pointed. There stood Mouse, leaning over and slobbering on Rufus, who lay on his back, paws in the air and squirming all over as if he'd just been given the best present in the world. He raised his head and licked Mouse across the face, in spite of the drool dripping from the big dog's jaws. Mouse seemed to grin all over, and he planted his foot on Rufus's belly and leaned down to lick him back.

Kate watched the dogs for a minute, then turned her gaze on Colt. "They're friends?" The last word came out with a squeak. "How did that happen? Why isn't Rufus fighting him?"

He shrugged. "I have no idea. I saw Rufus coming at a run from the corner of the house. None of you went that direction. I leaned over to pick Pete up, and he wrapped his arms around Mouse's neck so tight that I couldn't get him loose. He kept saying 'my friend, my friend' over and over. Rufus slammed to a stop a yard away and growled, then took a look at Pete hugging Mouse and rolled onto his back. Pete let go of Mouse, and the two dogs have been having a lickfest ever since."

Kate's mom grabbed Pete's hand to pull him toward her, but he jerked it loose and shook his head. He knelt by the dogs and put one hand on each of their heads and smiled.

"I can't believe it." She knelt beside Pete. "Honey, these two dogs don't know each other. Kate will tie up Rufus while Mouse is here."

"No!" He patted both dogs again. "Mouse is Pete's friend, Rufus is Pete's friend. Rufus is Mouse's friend." He pointed to the spot beside his leg, then told the big dog, "Sit, Mouse. Come here. Sit."

The dog took one step toward him and plunked his bottom down on the exact spot where Pete pointed. Rufus rolled over onto his belly, placed his head on his extended paws, and sighed.

"See? Mouse and Rufus are good dogs."

Kate almost choked over the tears welling in her throat. "Mom?"

Moisture coated her mother's cheeks. "I know, honey. I know. It's the most he's spoken at once in quite a while. And all because of this dog."

Jake moved toward Mouse, his eyes wide. He pointed at Pete. "I want this kid to train my dog. He knows what he's doing, all right!"

Thirty minutes later, Mouse's short training session was complete, with Pete having led the way on the first lesson in sitting. Kate was amazed that the big puppy listened to her little brother but rarely noticed anyone else. Now if only Jake could have the same success with Mouse, he'd be set. They sat around the kitchen table, Pete with a dog on each side, a hand stroking each head.

Jake stood nearby, bouncing on his toes. Kate shook her head. The kid hardly ever held still. "Hey, Jake. You want to stay a little longer? You probably need to call your dad and let him know."

"Affirmative. Roger that. Where's the phone?" He used his index finger to slide his glasses up on his nose while glancing around the room. "Should I tell him we're still working with Mouse?"

Kate's mom set a plate of cookies on the table. "Yes, Jake, I think you should."

Tori carried a tray with glasses and a pitcher of milk. Melissa smiled. "Thanks. This looks great."

"Did Mr. Wallace enjoy the cookies you kids took over to his house?" Kate's mom settled into a chair and turned her attention on Kate.

"Uh … yeah. He ate almost all of them before we left. I've never seen a man so excited about cookies."

"Good. Here you go, Jake. Help yourself." Kate's mom held out the plate so the newcomer could take one. "Pete, you can't feed them to the dogs."

He didn't reply but popped another piece into his own mouth.

Jake squatted in front of Mouse and looked up at Pete. "So you want to help me train Mouse to roll over and stay and all that stuff, Pete? He listens to you real good. Kind of like the Saint Bernard in the movie *Beethoven*, who adopted the Newton family and helped the kids. Only you helped him, Pete, instead of him helping you. Good job!" He held up his hand in front of Pete. "Give me a high five, fella!"

Everyone in the room held their breath as Pete raised his gaze to the level of Jake's hand and slowly met the boy's palm with his own, then put it back on Mouse's head.

"Wow!" Kate breathed the word, but Jake heard it and swiveled, his brows puckered.

"Wow, what? Did I do something wrong?"

She shook her head. "No way. You don't get it, do you?"

He shoved his glasses up. "Uh … no. Please elaborate."

"My little brother is autistic. He has a tutor who works with him, and he's improving, but he rarely talks as much as he did outside, and he's never given anyone a high five, or even allowed a stranger to touch him. What happened today is over-the-top cool."

"Oh." Jake's eyes rounded. "Yeah. That *is* cool. Maybe I should tell my parents that Mouse isn't so bad after all, and they shouldn't get rid of him."

Kate's mom sucked in a breath. "I'll tell your parents as well. I've met your mother, and she's a sensible woman. I think she'll change her mind when she hears how Pete responded to Mouse."

She smiled. "Don't you kids have more planning to do on the scavenger hunt?"

Colt nodded. "And we should work on that." He jerked his head toward the barn. "Let's check out hiding places in the barn and around the property. Want to help, Jake?"

"Most assuredly. Absolutely. You bet! Hiding places, huh? Did you ever see the movie *The Hiding Place*? It's one of my mom's favorites."

Colt grabbed Jake by the shoulder and gave him a gentle shove toward the door. "Let's go, dude. We've got work to do."

Kate's mom chuckled. "Mouse and Rufus can keep Pete company while you kids work on the hunt."

They left the house and walked to the barn. Jake stopped and looked around. "Splendid. Outstanding. Remarkable. This would make a great movie theater. Of course, you'd have to add top acoustics, seats, and a giant screen, but I can totally envision it." He held up his hands with his fingers framing the shape of a square and peered through, moving them from point to point in the arena. "But you guys haven't told me anything about a scavenger hunt. Are some of you hiding clues and the rest of us finding them?"

Kate sighed. "Sorry, Jake. We forgot you didn't know. Let's talk for a minute before we start finding places to hide items." She headed toward the room where they kept shavings and bales of straw and swung the door open. "Let's sit." She waited until everyone had taken a seat, then perched on the end of the bale where Tori and Melissa sat. "Colt, why don't you explain to Jake?" She tried to put meaning into her glance and hoped Colt caught it. They couldn't forget the real reason they'd invited Jake over, even if it had turned out to be great that he brought Mouse and Pete loved him.

Colt grabbed a piece of straw and placed it between his teeth. "Happy to. So, Jake, it's like this. We're having a big trail ride soon. The entry fees go to benefit Pete and other kids with autism. There's a day camp at the end of the summer—it lasts for two weeks and helps kids with special needs. It has an emphasis on autism, but it's expensive. Business owners have donated some great prizes, and people have paid their entry fees, so now all we have to do is figure out the items people will find, write down the clues, and hide the items."

Jake jumped to his feet. "Fantastico! Let's get at it, then. I'm a master at clues. I used to watch *Murder, She Wrote* all the time when I was a little kid, and I always solved the mystery before the star did."

Colt hauled Jake back down onto the bale of straw. "Whoa there, cowboy. Not so fast. There's more, and it has to do with your big brother."

"Jerry?" Jake's voice cracked on the word. "What about him?"

Colt winced. "Sorry. I'm getting ahead of myself. First, we didn't tell you that an antique box belonging to Kate's mom was stolen from the office. It contained a lot of the entry fees, and most of them were paid in cash. We're trying to figure out how to catch the thief and get our money back, so more kids have a chance to go to camp."

"No problemo. Jerry, huh?" He squinted and stroked his chin as though sporting a beard.

Kate could almost envision his glasses turning into a round eyeglass covering one eye and a pipe protruding from his lips. He just needed a hat to make him look like an old British detective. She giggled, then caught herself and sobered.

Jake stared at her. "So you think it's Jerry? He came over here with two of his friends so his girlfriend could sign up, didn't he?"

Melissa leaned forward. "That was his girlfriend?"

Jake shrugged. "I suppose. Lisa is a girl, and she must not be his enemy, or he wouldn't have brought her." He waved his hand in the air. "Now back to your investigative quandary."

Tori wrinkled her nose. "Our what?"

"Your mystery. You're trying to solve 'the mystery of the missing box.' You want my help. I am considered something of a genius when it comes to mysteries, so you've come to the right man." His voice squeaked on the last word, and it was all Kate could do not to giggle again, but she didn't want to hurt his feelings.

Colt worked the piece of straw to the other side of his mouth. "Let's hear it. What kind of ideas do you have?"

"So why do you think Jerry might be your culprit? Did you see him with the box?"

Melissa shook her head. "No, but he noticed it when they were in the office. We made a list of several people who did, and we're pretty sure we ruled out one man already. We need to figure out who the real thief is, if possible."

He gave a curt nod. "Right-o. It's very possible. Jerry had sticky fingers in the past."

Tori gasped. "He's stolen from other people?"

Jake sighed. "In all fairness, it was a piece of candy at the store when he was eight. My mother still hangs it over his head when she gets mad at him for something. But I know he stole another guy's girlfriend once. It does show a proclivity to crime, don't you think?"

Kate stared at Jake, not sure she understood. "Um … proclivity? Want to explain?"

He gave an eager nod. "Sure. It means tendency. Penchant. Aptitude. Bent. I could go on if you want."

"No. I'm good." She grinned. "Thanks. I have a feeling we'll learn a lot with you around." But Kate stuffed down disappointment. She'd thought they might get some actual help from this kid about his brother, but stealing a piece of candy and a girlfriend? "Maybe we're wrong. Just because Jerry noticed the box doesn't mean he took it. Thanks for trying, Jake."

He held up his hand and blinked behind his thick lenses. "Let's not be hasty, people. We must investigate every suspect, no matter how slim the chance he absconded with the goods. It's time to set up a sting, a ruse, a trap for my big brother that he can't resist."

"Great!" Colt pumped his fist in the air. "Now you're talking, Jake. What do you have in mind?"

"Not a thing. I simply came up with the brilliant idea to set a trap, and it's up to you to implement what that might be."

Melissa groaned. "This is going nowhere."

Tori nodded. "We already tried to trap the thief, Jake. We put out word that we had more money in the office, hoping to lure him back here. No one showed up. So that won't work if it's Jerry."

"All right." He crossed his arms over his bony chest. "Then we'll take the war to him."

Chapter Fifteen

The following morning, Kate and her four friends stood outside Jake's house and looked at the upstairs window.

Kate sucked in a long breath. "You sure this will work, Jake? Do you think Jerry's going to leave?"

Jake gave an emphatic nod. "Affirmative. He's not going to let his girlfriend hang if he thinks she needs help." He winked. "Not if he doesn't want one of the other college jocks moving in on his territory."

Colt motioned Jake toward the front door. "All right, then, let's do this. Remember, we have to be quick. We don't know how much time Jake can buy us."

"Right." Kate followed Jake up the sidewalk, with Tori and Melissa on either side. "And you're sure your parents aren't home?"

"Positive. Mom is shopping in Portland, and Dad is at work. It's Saturday, but he's working overtime. He gave me permission to ride my bike to your house, but Jerry is supposed to be watching me." He wrinkled his nose. "Good grief. I'm older and as smart as Kevin in *Home Alone*, and I don't need anybody babysitting me—especially somebody irresponsible like Jerry."

He pushed the door and stepped inside, holding it open for the rest of them to enter, then closed it. Walking to the base of the staircase, he hollered, "Hey, Jerry. You need to come down here."

Silence.

"Jerry! I have a message for you."

Nothing.

Tori looked at Kate and Melissa, and Kate shrugged. "Maybe he isn't home. He could have left after you did, Jake."

"Negatory. Of course, Lisa's house is only three blocks away, so he could have gone over there, but Dad told him he had to stay home and get his messy room picked up or else. Jerry didn't like it. He thinks he's a big man now that he's in college, but Dad told him to clean it up or move out, vamoose, depart. Dad's sick of not being able to open the door if he needs to go in there. If Jerry doesn't finish before Dad gets home, he's dead meat."

Jake stopped beside a mahogany table with a mirror placed above it and scooped up a set of car keys. "We can't have him driving to Lisa's. He'd get back here too fast. Colt, will you keep these in case he tries to search me? I wouldn't put it past him. We'll return them after he leaves."

Colt pocketed the keys. "So now what? Go up and get him?"

Jake grinned. "This never fails. Hey, Jerry! Message from Lisa!"

Feet thudded on the floor above, and a door opened and slammed shut. Jerry charged down the stairs and stopped halfway, staring at Jake. "What's up, shrimp? And who are your friends?" He glanced at Colt for an instant. Then his gaze slid over Tori and Kate and lingered on Melissa. "I haven't seen *you* around."

She smirked at him. "That's because I'm in middle school, and you're in college."

His face reddened. "Oh." He pivoted toward Jake. "What were you yelling about Lisa? I didn't hear the phone ring."

"You never hear anything with your music on and your door closed," Jake countered. "It's a good thing I came in when I did. She wants you over at her house pronto. She has something she needs to move, and she asked if I could come too."

Jerry eyed him. "You? That's weird. You don't have a single muscle in your entire body." He bolted down the rest of the stairs and stopped in front of the hall table. "I left my car keys here. They're gone."

Jake crossed his arms. "Man, you're worse than the character on—"

Jerry cuffed Jake on the back of his head. "Snap out of it, shrimp. No one wants to hear your movie analogies. Just give me my keys."

"I don't have them." Jake rubbed his head. "You're worse than Gibbs on *NCIS* when it comes to slapping heads. Find your own keys. Better yet, keep making your girlfriend wait. Walk the whole three blocks." He jerked open the door. "And I'll beat you there and tell her you hit me."

He bolted down the front steps, with Jerry on his heels, bellowing the entire way. "Go home, Jake. I can get there by myself, and I don't want you helping Lisa with anything."

Tori peered out the open door. "Do you think Jake will be okay? Yikes. It looks like Jerry sent him back, but he's moving slow."

Colt grinned. "That little kid is smart. He just bought us the time we need. Besides, I'm not crazy about snooping in Jerry's room and having his parents return without Jake here. Now let's get going before Jerry gets back." He raced up the stairs, with the girls following.

As soon as they reached the upper hallway, they stopped and stared. Kate turned in a slow circle. "Did Jake happen to mention which room is Jerry's? I don't want to barge into their parents' room."

Colt nodded. "Jake said his is the first door on the right; then the bathroom. Jerry's is across on the left. Their parents' room is in the other direction." He moved forward, then stopped in front of the door on the left. "Remember, anything you move, put back where you found it, and don't touch anything that's too small to hide the box." He turned the knob and swung open the door. "If we find the box and it's empty, then we'll have to look for the cash."

Kate peered around him. "What a disaster!" If only she had Mom's latex gloves that she used to clean the bathroom. And maybe a dust mask. Ugh. She moved into the room slowly, taking in the chaos. Blankets were on the floor, old food sat on the nightstand, discarded clothing littered most surfaces, and an unpleasant odor permeated the room. She held her nose and breathed through her mouth. "No wonder his dad said he had to clean his room. This is disgusting."

Melissa tiptoed over a rotted apple core not far from the bed. "Gross. I don't even know where to start."

Tori stood inside the door and stared around the room. "I don't think it matters if we move anything. I can't imagine Jerry would notice. But whatever we do, we'd better get busy before he gets here."

Kate navigated her way to the window. "I'm going to open this for now. Maybe it'll make it more bearable while we look." She grabbed the frame and pushed it up as far as it would go, then took a big gulp of air. "Much better." She leaned out and waved. "Hey, Jake. You on the lookout for us?"

"Yeah. I'll whistle if I see Jerry, and I'll try to stall him. But you'd better hurry. He might figure out I sent him on a wild-goose chase and come running."

They spent the next few minutes carefully opening drawers, looking in the closet, and picking up dirty clothes tossed over objects on the dresser and floor. Colt even stooped to peer under the bed but quickly jumped to his feet. "I won't even tell you what's under there. Ugh."

After ten minutes of searching, Tori dusted her hands against her jeans. "I haven't seen anything close to your mom's box, Kate. How about the rest of you?"

Melissa shook her head. "Nothing. And I feel like I need a hot shower. This room is so gross."

Kate plucked another dirty shirt off the floor from behind the closet door, then dropped it where she found it. "What do you think? Have we looked enough, or do we keep searching?"

Colt pressed his lips together. "Jake thought his brother might have the box, but I'm starting to feel kinda stupid for coming. The only place we didn't search is the closet. I know if I was going to hide something important, I'd put it under my bed or as far into the closet as I could—either on the floor where it's dark or on the shelf behind something else."

Melissa sighed. "So do you want to tackle it, Colt? Kate and I had our share of dark, dirty places when we went up in Mrs. Maynard's attic. I'm willing to let you take this one."

Tori bit her lip. "I suppose I could help." She turned beseeching eyes on Colt. "If you need me, that is?"

"Naw. I think I can swing it." He stepped over to the large closet that wasn't quite a walk-in and pushed all the hangers with clothes to one side. Bending over, he peered into the corner, then repeated the action on the other side. "That only leaves the top shelf."

Kate grabbed the wooden chair in front of the desk and dragged it to him. "This might make it easier."

He climbed up on the chair and reached as far as he could to one side, moving a box out of the way.

All of a sudden, Jake's whistle penetrated the room, and Kate whirled toward the open window. "Oh no! Is Jerry back?" She slid across to the side of the window and peeked out. Jake stood between Jerry and the front door, waving his hands in his brother's face.

Chapter Sixteen

Kate ran to the chair where Colt balanced as he struggled to return a bag to the closet shelf. She tugged on his shirttail. "You've got to hurry, or we're going to get caught." She glanced at the window and groaned. "Should I try to shut the window with them out there? Jake's doing his best to keep Jerry outside."

Jerry's shout echoed through the room. "Get out of my way, shrimp! I got to Lisa's, and she said she never spoke to you. What are you trying to pull?"

Jake's high-pitched reply reached Kate and her friends clearly. "Just give me a minute to explain, okay? Why are you in such a rush to go in and clean your room? It's not like you ever cared before now."

"And why do you want to keep me out here, huh? What happened to your nerdy little friends? Did you send them home, or are they casing the joint and robbing us blind?"

Colt moved the final item on the far right side of the closet shelf and looked behind it, then grunted. He jumped off the chair and returned it to the desk. "Slide the window shut fast, Melissa. There's not a thing here. We'd better get out of here pronto."

Tori was shaking, and Melissa slid the window closed, then crossed to the open door. She teetered on her toes. "Come on, come on!" She whispered the words and waved her hand. "Move it! I heard them come through the front door."

They tiptoed to the door and into the hall. Melissa looked both ways, then dashed for the room Jake had said was the bathroom, slipping inside as heavy feet thudded up the stairs.

Tori stared at the closing door, her lips parted. "What's she doing? Leaving us to take the rap alone?"

Colt softly pulled Jerry's bedroom door shut and took a step toward the stairway, right as Jerry burst into sight on the landing, with Jake on his heels.

Jerry balled his fists and raised them. "Busted! I caught you all in the act."

Jake slipped around his older brother and stood by Colt. "What are you talking about, Jerry? They're just standing here minding their own business."

Jerry laughed, and it wasn't pleasant. "Right. The cops aren't gonna believe that when I tell them they've been in our house alone, and I found them upstairs snooping."

Jake looked at Kate and barely raised his brows. She gave a slight shake of her head.

Jerry stared from one to the other. "Hey, what gives? Jake, is this your girlfriend? You trying to sneak her upstairs?"

Jake rolled his eyes. "Whatever. I told them they could wait for me in the house until I got back. And if you remember, you told me to go home, so I've been here the whole time. Quit making a humongous deal out of everything."

Jerry planted his fists at his waist. "You and your stupid words. I find your friends upstairs where they don't belong, and you hanging around outside like you were watching for me. *That's* the big deal."

The bathroom door opened, and Melissa stepped out, tossing her head. She stopped as though startled, then smiled at Jerry. "You're back! How nice. I'm so sorry I took so long in the bathroom and made everyone else wait. Tori, it's your turn next, right?"

Tori nodded, then dashed into the room and shut the door behind her with a click.

Jerry looked from one to the other. "You telling me you're up here to use the can? What's wrong with the one downstairs?"

Colt leaned his shoulder against the wall. "Jake told us the bathroom was upstairs right next to his room, and we could wait in his room if we wanted to. So we all came up, then I guess we needed to use it at the same time. We'll hurry if you want it next, Jerry." He straightened and raised his hand to rap on the door.

Jerry stepped toward his room and glowered. "Forget it. I didn't say anything about needing the can. Jake, you and your little clown friends better hurry up and get outta here. They've overstayed their welcome, if you ask me." He opened his door, went inside, then slammed it behind him, making the walls shake.

Jake jumped, then motioned toward the bathroom. "Kate, tell Tori to come out," he whispered.

Kate gave a gentle tap on the door, and Tori cracked it open. "Is it safe?"

"Yes. Let's get out of here." Kate headed for the steps behind Colt and Jake, with Tori and Melissa following. That had been too close, and they hadn't even found the box. But at least they hadn't ended up in jail or been tossed to the bottom of the stairwell by Jerry.

They trooped to the first level, then out the front door. Jake led them for a full block before he stopped and turned. "So you didn't find the object of our search? Did you turn over every stone and look in every crack and crevice?"

Melissa sighed. "We picked up every piece of dirty clothes and rotted food and dirty plates, if that's what you mean. Sorry, Jake. If your brother is guilty of taking the box, it's not in his room. Colt even poked into the back corners of the closet and under the bed."

Colt nodded. "Yeah. Not fun, let me tell you. Does that guy ever do laundry or take a bath? Man, that room is gross, and I thought mine was bad. Jerry's makes mine look like a neat freak lives there."

Jake laughed and shoved his glasses up the bridge of his nose. "He cleans up pretty good when he has a date. Now you can see why my dad told him to clean his room or *hasta la vista*, adios, farewell, he's outta here! My parents are sick of the stench."

They walked along the road toward Kate's house, and Jake kicked a large rock out of the way, then winced and hopped on one foot. "So what's next, huh? Do we go all James Bond again on the next suspect? Not that I've seen those Bond films, but I've seen every *Spy Kids* movie, and I've got a lot of great ideas we could use."

Tori held up her hand. "I don't know about the rest of you, but I think we've done enough snooping for the day. Maybe we need to find places to hide stuff around the barn and on the property, then walk the trail again and make notes on other good hiding spots."

Melissa grabbed a handful of leaves as she walked under a low-hanging branch. "I agree with Tori. Kate's mom put ads all over the place about her box. Maybe the person who took it will bring it back."

"Doubtful," said Jake. "Now if we only lived back in pirate days, we could make Jerry walk the plank, like in *Pirates of the Caribbean*. I'll bet we could even get a confession out of him!" He rubbed his hands together and chuckled.

Colt sighed. "Problem is, we don't have a suspect we can make walk the plank. Right now we're no better off than when we started. I agree with Tori. Let's go to the barn and do some figuring. You need to get Mouse anyway, Jake. Want to help us?"

"Unequivocally. Unmistakably. Absolutely." He nodded. "We could use Mouse to scout the area and make sure the coast is clear before we go in to reconnoiter."

Kate sighed but managed a smile. "I think he needs a little more training before that happens, Jake. But nice idea." She turned into their driveway and headed to the barn. "At least we're home, and there won't be any more surprises or rude people yelling at us."

Thirty minutes later Jake picked up a rock that was holding down the corner of a tarp covering some straw. He waved a folded paper in the air. "Hey, guys. I didn't know you'd already started hiding clues."

The four of them rushed over to the boy, and Kate leaned over. "We haven't hidden anything yet, and we won't hide clues. We'll hide stuff they have to bring back. I was the last one to take straw out from under this tarp yesterday, and I know there wasn't anything there when I covered it." She picked up the folded paper. "Anyone know anything about this?"

"Nope." An echo of replies sounded around the group.

Melissa stared at Kate. "You going to just stand there or open it? It's not like it blew under that rock. Someone had to put it there."

"True." Kate unfolded the paper and let her gaze run over it; then she gasped.

"What?" A chorus of voices hit her.

She gazed at it again, then turned it around so they could see it.

Colt took a step closer. "No way! This has to be from the thief."

Tori shuddered. "And he took a picture of the box and put it here to taunt us? What's with that?"

Melissa held out her hand. "May I see it?"

Kate handed it over. "He says he wants to make things right, but I'm not sure of the rest. All I could do was stare at the picture of Mom's box. Why don't you read it out loud, Melissa?"

"Good idea." Melissa took a deep breath, then exhaled. "I am so ashamed I took your box, but I can't come forward publicly and return it. Think of this as a treasure hunt—one you can do on your own before the real scavenger hunt begins. Go to the north pasture at the base of the corner post." She lowered the paper, her lips parted and eyes wide.

"Radical!" Jake shouted, making them all jump. "So what are we standing here for? Let's go find us some treasure! I feel like one of the people in *National Treasure* trying to outmaneuver the bad guys. Come on, Kate, it's your pasture. Lead the way!"

Kate's heart pounded hard. "I've never seen *National Treasure*, but that sounds good to me—as long as there aren't any bad guys waiting for us."

Tori stood along with the rest of the group. "Do you think it's safe?"

Colt grinned. "I doubt there's anything waiting in the pasture besides manure piles, grass, and fence posts. But there's only one way to find out. Let's go!"

Chapter Seventeen

The five of them raced across the pasture, with Jake bringing up the rear. Kate's long legs almost kept pace with Colt, but he reached the north side of the pasture right before she did. He skidded to a halt. "Hey, which corner? He only said north side and the corner, but there are two corners."

Jake panted to a stop. "You mean we aren't there yet? That was a long way already. How big is this field anyway?"

Kate smiled. "You need to watch less TV and get out more, Jake. It's twenty acres." She pivoted and pointed to the right. "That's the closest corner. Should we all go that way or split up so we can check both corners at once?"

"Split up," Colt said in a determined tone.

"Stay here and rest," Jake sank onto the grass.

Melissa snorted. "Is that what the Spy Kids would do? Or Indiana Jones, or even Kevin in *Home Alone* when he was setting all those traps? Come on, Jake, you can't find treasure sitting around. You've got to be adventurous like the kids in *The Hunger Games*."

"My parents didn't allow me to watch *The Hunger Games*. They said it's too dark for kids. I mostly watch the old movies and TV shows."

Tori narrowed her eyes and scanned the entire pasture. "There's four of us without Jake. Let's split up. Jake can sit here, and the team that finds it can holler for the others to come running."

Jake struggled to his feet. "I'll come, if you don't mind me going with the team that has the shortest distance to cover."

"Whatever." Melissa flipped her hair over her shoulder. "Colt, want to race me to the far corner?" She took off without waiting for an answer.

Colt shrugged. "Girls." He followed her at a ground-eating lope.

Kate laughed. "His legs are so much longer, he'll catch her even with her head start. And they're going to beat us if we don't get with it." She pivoted, then dashed toward the closer corner, with Tori and Jake not far behind.

They knelt at the post and ran their hands through the grass. Kate slumped in disappointment. "There's no box here."

Tori frowned. "Maybe Colt and Melissa will find it."

Jake sighed. "So we have to walk all the way across this pasture to the other post?"

"No," Kate said. "They'll probably meet us halfway. We should be able to see if they're carrying it before they get to us." She pushed to her feet. "Don't worry. We won't make you run again."

They walked at a brisk pace toward the other post and met Colt and Melissa just over halfway. Neither had the box. Colt dug his hand in his pocket and withdrew a paper. "He left another clue instead of the box."

Disappointment hit Kate hard. She'd so hoped this would be the end of the mystery, and even if they didn't find out who took the box, they'd have it and the entry money back. "Great. Did you read it?"

Colt nodded and glanced at Melissa. "But we're not sure where to go from here."

Jake held out his hand. "I'm good at puzzles. Want me to give it a try?"

"Sure." Colt handed it over.

Jake shoved his glasses up on his nose. "Let's see. Hmm. Right. Okay."

Melissa huffed. "Hey. Out loud. Everyone will want to hear it."

"Ah, pardon my poor manners." Jake grinned. "Here goes. 'If you've found this, then you're halfway to your treasure. Go to the path that leads to the big tree, and tangled in the roots, you'll find what you seek.'" Jake looked up. "Sounds pretty simple to me. So where's this big tree?"

Colt shrugged. "All we could figure out is the tree we found on our trail ride with the roots that stick up above the ground. There was a pretty deep pocket beneath it where he might have been able to put the box."

Jake groaned. "More running?"

Kate sighed. "Afraid so. But we don't have to run the entire way. We'll walk part of it."

They trudged across the pasture and up the road to where the path took off through the woods. Colt led as they fell into single file. "Keep your eyes open, in case it's not that tree."

They walked in silence, then almost tiptoed the last several yards to the tree. Kate held her breath, hoping they'd find the box and all the money as well. Funny that the note hadn't said anything about returning the money, just the box. Of course, the thief didn't have the key, but she'd assumed he'd have destroyed the lock by now and taken the cash.

They formed a semicircle around the tree. Tori leaned closer. "I don't see anything. Should we check under the roots in case he shoved it farther back?"

Jake flapped his hands in the air. "Danger alert! Danger alert! Haven't you seen movies where rats and bats and snakes and all sorts of creatures lurk in dark hidey-holes and spring out at you when you least expect it?"

Melissa tensed. "I hate rats and bats. And spiders." She shuddered. "I'm not sticking my hands under there. No way." She took a step back.

"I'm not scared of snakes," Jake said, "but I wish we'd brought Mouse. He'd root out anything bad."

Kate planted her hands on her hips. "I thought you told us he's afraid of mice."

"He is. But a bat isn't a mouse, and no rats have raced out yet."

Colt dropped to his knees and probed the area beneath the roots. "Nothing!"

"What?" Kate joined him, not caring how many creatures might jump out at her. The box had to be there! "My hands are smaller than yours. Let me try. I might be able to get farther in. Did you feel another note?"

"Nope." Colt waited for her to try, but she came up empty as well. "Now what?" He rocked back on his heels.

Melissa moaned. "I'm out of ideas."

"There's got to be another big tree with roots that we haven't thought of yet." Tori rounded on Kate. "Would it be one of the trees in your yard?"

Kate slapped her forehead. "Why didn't I think of that? The huge pine has roots that stick up. I don't think you could hide the box there, but a note for sure." She spun around and jogged up the trail, knowing her friends would follow.

It didn't take long to reach her yard, and Kate hurried to the tree. She sank to the ground and felt along each root. Colt arrived at the spot, along with the rest of her friends. "Anything?"

"Not yet."

Melissa eased down beside Kate. "I don't know what to think. Either there has to be another tree we haven't checked, or this guy is playing games."

Jake bounced from one foot to the other. "I agree. I was watching—"

Colt laid a hand on Jake's shoulder. "Sorry, dude, but that's not helping right now. We need to figure out what to do. That box of money is pretty important to the kids who want to go to camp."

"Affirmative. Assuredly. Got it. Sorry." Jake's posture sagged and he slumped to the ground.

Tori sat next to him and gave him a shoulder bump. "It's all cool, Jake. And sometimes your movie analogies are funny. I kinda like them."

His face brightened. "Really?" A tiny dimple showed in his cheek when his grin broadened. "You should come over and watch—"

Tori laughed and poked him in the ribs. "Not now, Jake."

"Oh. Right. My apologies yet again."

Colt squatted beside Kate. "I hate to give up."

"Me too. We need to keep thinking. Maybe there's another big tree nearby. The thief obviously knows about one we don't, so let's keep our eyes open anytime we ride our bikes."

Melissa nodded. "Or when we're placing the items for the trail ride." She snapped her fingers. "Did you guys realize that the trail ride is next weekend? We'd better get busy and finalize our plans."

Kate leaned against the tree. "Everything is basically done except placing the items. Between the clues we wrote, ones Mom and her two horse-club-leader friends wrote, and some Dad wrote, we're all done with those. And Mom and Dad went together to the store to buy the items with the money we got when we opened registration again for another two days. The only thing left is for us to hide the items." She whacked her fist against the tree. "It makes me sick that this guy is playing games. Do you suppose it's Mr. Wallace getting even with us for snooping in his house and knocking over his magazine and newspaper piles?"

Jake snorted a laugh. "I'd say the same about Jerry, but I don't think he's smart enough to think up something like this."

Tori looked from face to face. "There were a couple of other people we haven't checked into yet. Should we at least go to Mr. Creighton's business or Mr. Addington's and see what we can find out?"

Melissa shook her head. "Do we really have time? We've got a lot of stuff to hide before the ride."

Jake perked up. "I like it. I say we do it. What do we have to lose except an hour or two?"

Colt tore up a handful of grass and let it filter through his fingers. "What are you suggesting?"

Jake blew out a breath. "My brain is frozen. No connection. Sheesh." He slapped his forehead. "Guess I shouldn't have said anything."

Kate thought for a moment. "Mr. Creighton's store is closest. Let's browse through the store like we plan to buy something."

Melissa frowned. "It's not like it's going to be on a shelf for sale. What do you hope to find?"

"I don't know, but it's a place to start."

"I agree," Colt said. "We can ride our bikes over there in ten minutes. Do you need to tell your mom we're going, Kate?"

"Yeah. I'll run in and do that right now. Hey! Jake doesn't have his bike here." She looked at Colt. "Your legs are longer. Want to ride my dad's bike and let Jake ride yours?"

"Sure."

Fifteen minutes later they sat on their bikes outside the electronics store. Nobody moved. Colt rubbed his chin. "He might not even be here."

"All the better," Kate said. "We can look around without being suspected, if he *is* the thief."

They parked their bikes and headed inside. Kate's pulse pounded in her ears. She hoped no one would do anything stupid that would get them in trouble, but with the poor success rate they'd had so far, she wasn't going to count anything out.

Chapter Eighteen

Kate and Tori stood in the open doorway of the store office.

Tori nudged Kate. "What if someone catches us standing here looking around?" She glanced over her shoulder toward their three friends, who were talking to a clerk.

Kate craned her neck to see farther into the room. "Colt said they'll keep anyone busy who tries to get near the office. It's not like we're going to touch anything, and besides, the door was wide open."

"I suppose. So do we just stand here and hope we spot the box?"

Kate edged into the room another half step. "I'd like to be able to see behind the desk. It looks like a set of shelves there." She took another step.

Tori grabbed her arm. "Hold it," she whispered. "We'll get busted big-time if Mr. Creighton comes back."

Kate hesitated, knowing her friend was right. They had no business snooping in this man's private office, but if he didn't want anyone looking in here, he should keep the door closed. That led to another thought, and she slumped. "Do you suppose he'd leave the door open if he'd hidden a stolen box here?"

Tori blew out a loud breath. "No way. Come on. We'd better leave. I don't see anything anyway."

Kate held up her hand. "Hold it. I've got an idea." She peered behind her into the store and raised her voice. "Mr. Creighton? We were hoping to talk to you." She noticed a door on the far side of the office in the corner. Why hadn't she seen that before? Great. What if he came out now while she was in the office? She sucked in a lungful of air. "Mr. Creighton? Are you here?"

The corner door whipped open, and Mr. Creighton stepped through the open doorway into his office, then closed the door firmly behind him. "What are you girls doing in here?" He pointed to the door they'd come through. "Didn't you see the sign? It says 'Private.'"

Kate winced. They were done for. "No, sir. The door was wide open, and the sign must be on the other side, so we didn't notice it. We're sorry."

He crossed his arms. "What do you want?"

Kate heard a noise outside the room and peered around Tori. Colt, Melissa, and Jake stood there, mouths agape and fear in their eyes. She swung back to Mr. Creighton, thinking fast.

"We're so sorry to bother you. Is your daughter excited about the trail ride? Does she have any questions we can help with?"

The man relaxed and let his arms drop to his sides. "Oh. Well. Thank you for asking. I think she has all the information she needs. When is it? Next weekend?"

Kate nodded. "Yes, sir. It starts at ten o'clock on Saturday morning. I remember you said she's not an advanced rider and hasn't done this kind of hunt before. We'll be helping anyone who needs it. There should be a really good turnout, so you can trailer her horse in early if you'd like to."

"Fine. We may do that." He smiled. "Anything else I can help with?"

She paused, wondering if she dared ask her next question. "Well ... we've been looking for a really big tree with roots that pop up above the ground where something can be hidden. You know. For the scavenger hunt. A tree that would stand out. Do you happen to know of any like that?" She watched him closely.

"Hmm ... can't say that I do. But if I notice one, I'll give you a call, how's that?" He walked to his desk and pulled out his chair. "Now I really must get busy. If you'll excuse me?" He smiled but dipped his head toward the doorway.

"Oh. Sure. Thanks. And again, we're sorry for bothering you. Have a nice day." She backed out of the room, with Tori close beside her. They headed for the front of the store with their three friends following, not one of them saying a word.

They stepped outside and walked a half block before Jake exploded. "Brilliant! Mastermind! Bravo, Kate!"

Melissa scowled at him. "What are you talking about? Half the time I can't figure you out."

Jake stopped and stared. "Simple, maestro. Kate dropped that genius question on him about the tree out of left field, to see how he'd react. If he'd stumbled around and acted guilty, then we'd know he was the one who left the clues."

"Right," Tori said. "But he didn't act guilty. So I'm not sure what it gained us to take the risk of going into his office."

Colt motioned them forward. "Let's get back to Kate's house. All this investigating has left me hungry and thirsty. I think Jake's right. He didn't act guilty, so we might be able to rule him out as a suspect. Plus, he was awfully nice about Kate and Tori being in his office."

Melissa shrugged. "So he fell for what they said about his daughter. It's not like they said it's the reason we came."

"Right," Colt nodded. "Or he might have been nice to hide the fact that he's the thief. Short of barging into that back room and searching it and his house, I don't think there's any more we can do."

The following Saturday morning arrived way too fast for Kate's liking. She was excited about the trail ride and scavenger hunt, but she was having a hard time getting over the sense of loss and disappointment they'd all been dealing with since her mom's box disappeared.

So far today, they'd checked in all the riders, given them numbers, and handed them sheets with the clues scrambled. That way there wouldn't be riders running over each other at the same location. Kate and her friends had spent the past two days setting up the course. They'd decided on three different trails: one for young riders who were beginners, and two for advanced and intermediate riders. Now it was time to ride out and check on the progress since all the hunters had left the barn.

Tori stopped beside her. "Do you think we did enough? I hope the horses won't spook at some of the stops we came up with—like that bag of golf balls hanging from a tree."

"The riders can get off their horses and lead them up to it to get a ball if they need to."

Melissa giggled. "It was pretty cute what you wrote: 'You're going to be teed off at this clue. Go find what you need to tee off.'"

Colt grinned. "I liked the school-spirit one, with a letter-men's jacket hanging on a bush, and they have to find a 'letter.' I think we should have hung the bucket of wooden letters farther away, though. I'm afraid it's too easy."

Jake pushed his glasses up on his nose. "I still don't see how they're going to win prizes by finding the items from following the clues." He held Mouse's leash tighter as the dog started to pull away.

Kate tipped her head toward the barn. "Let's get saddled up. Jake, you and Mouse can keep an eye on things around the barn and the pastures, in case anyone has questions. The rest of us will ride out. To answer your question, we give every person who enters a set of clues to find different items. We hid twenty, but the first person in each age category to bring back ten items gets a prize. For example, with the golf balls, they'll follow the clue, and when they find the bag, they'll take only one ball. Each person has to bring back one of everything that the clues lead to. Then the second, third, and fourth persons in each category to bring back all the items get a prize too. The ones who come in first get their choice of the things donated before anyone else."

"Right." Jake jerked on Mouse's leash. "Maybe I should have Pete come with us. Mouse loves him and obeys him a lot better than me."

"Great idea." Kate waved at her mother, who was talking to the last person who'd arrived late. "Hey, Mom. Can Pete hang out with Mouse and Jake around the barn and pasture?"

"Sure, honey. That's a great idea." She knelt in front of Pete. "Want to go with Jake?"

He shook his head. "Want to go with Mouse. Not Jake. Rufus too." He reached out and took Rufus's leash, then trotted toward Jake. "Come, Rufus. Let's get Mouse."

Kate grinned. "I love how great he is with the dogs, and how it's been helping him to talk more."

Jake laughed. "And I love how much better behaved Mouse is since he met Pete. Mom and Dad said I can keep him if he behaves better."

He, Pete, and the two dogs headed toward the large outdoor arena. "We'll cut across and to the pasture. I saw a couple of people head out there."

"Good idea." Colt waved, and he and the girls walked to the barn. "Time to mount up and hit the trail. It's going to be interesting to see if everyone finds all the items we hid with the clues we gave them."

A horrible thought struck Kate, and she shivered. "What's the chance someone stumbles across the big tree with the exposed roots and finds our box?" Her hands intertwined with nervous energy. "I'm not sure if that would be good or terrible, depending on who found it and whether they returned it."

Melissa narrowed her eyes. "I was thinking about that too, but I don't believe the thief would have left it there. He would have come back and checked to see if we got it and taken it with him. I'm surprised we never heard from him again."

Tori frowned. "Maybe he decided he didn't feel so bad about stealing it after all and kept it. And if so, there goes most of our money."

Chapter Nineteen

Kate sat on Capri and watched the last riders turn in the items they'd found as they followed the clues on the hunt. Tori sat astride Starlight, while Melissa and Colt stood on the ground, holding the reins of their horses. Kate looked around. "Where's Jake?"

Colt jerked his head toward the house. "Pete refused to take a nap unless both Mouse and Rufus came along. Jake went to get them all settled so your mom could stay here and award the rest of the prizes."

Melissa grinned. "I wasn't sure about Jake at first, but he's a pretty good kid. Even with all his crazy movie analogies."

Tori giggled. "He makes me laugh."

Colt motioned them toward the barn. "Suppose we should put our horses up now? It feels like I've been riding all day, even though it's only been two or three hours."

Kate nodded. "Probably a good idea. It's pretty cool that one of the youngest riders found the most items in the little kids' age group, huh? She sure seemed to love the tickets to ride Thomas the Train when it comes through town again. That was a great idea to check with them, Melissa."

The other girl shrugged. "I got to ride it when I was a kid, and I remember how excited I was. It's awesome that it comes to Hood River in the summer."

Kate and Tori swung off their horses and walked behind Colt and Melissa toward the barn. They spent the next few minutes stripping off saddles and bridles and brushing their mounts. They put the horses in their stalls, then headed for the awards area outside.

Kate flipped her braid over her shoulder. "I'm almost too tired to care about the rest of the prizes. I'm glad Mom's taking care of it. Which ones do you think created the most excitement?"

Tori hop-skipped beside Kate to keep up with her longer stride. "I saw a guy who was pretty pumped about a set of ski-lift tickets for Mount Hood Meadows, and a lady who got super-excited about a gift certificate at a beauty salon. I don't think anyone was disappointed with the prizes they won."

Colt grabbed a piece of straw as he passed a bale and popped it between his lips. "I agree. All the hard work paid off. Or it would have, if the box hadn't been stolen. I guess at this point, all we can do is keep praying that God talks to the person who took it and convinces him to bring it back. That's what your dad told us to do, right?"

Someone behind them cleared his throat.

Kate slowed and looked over her shoulder. "Oh, hi, Mr. Creighton. Did your daughter win anything?"

"I'm afraid not, but that's all right. Her horse was a little lame, so I took them home early." He ran a hand through his hair.

Kate's friends faced the man, and Colt took a step toward him. "Is there something we can do for you, sir? I'm surprised you came back if your daughter is finished for the day."

"Actually, there is something wrong, but I'd rather talk to all of you and Kate's parents after everyone's left, if you have time. I don't want to intrude, though." He took a step toward the half-dozen cars and trucks with trailers still in the parking area. "Maybe I should forget this and come back another time."

What's wrong with him? Kate wondered. His face was pale, and he looked like he might hurl. Had his daughter's horse been hurt on their property, and would he sue them? Her heart skipped a beat. "Whatever it is, Mr. Creighton, I think my parents will want to hear about it today and not wait. Would you like to go into the office until they finish?"

He held up his hands, and if anything, his face got whiter. "No! Not there. I'll just sit on a bale of straw in the shade, if that's all right. Maybe you could let them know I'm here?"

"Sure." Kate tipped her head toward her friends. "Want to walk with me?"

Melissa glanced at Mr. Creighton. "Should we go home? You only want to talk to Kate and her parents, right?"

He shook his head. "No. All of you. Please. If you can stay, that is?"

Melissa eyed Tori and Colt. They all gave a single nod. "Sure," Melissa said. "We'll hang out until Kate's parents finish up." She raised a brow at Kate. "We probably should get Jake."

Kate nodded, then smiled at Mr. Creighton. "There's a table with chairs on the back patio of the house, if you'd like to wait there. I'll bring out something cold to drink."

"I don't want to be any bother. Please."

"It's not a bother. Mom and Dad will be hot and tired by the time they finish with the last contestant, and we are too. Go ahead. We'll catch up with you."

Fifteen minutes later, Kate, her friends, and her parents congregated on the back patio. Colt and Jake each took a dog leash and sank onto the grass not far from Pete.

Pete patted the ground beside him. "Come on, Rufus. Mouse. Sit by me." Both dogs obediently sank to their bellies, one on each side of Kate's little brother, their jowls pulled back in happy canine grins.

Kate reached out to touch Pete's hair, then hesitated, not knowing if he'd jerk away as he so often did, or simply ignore her. She'd been asking God to make Pete better for so long. Maybe God sent Mouse to help bring him out of himself and into the world where his family lived. She lightly touched his hair.

Pete shot a glance her direction but didn't hold it. "Kate." He pointed to the grass on the other side of Rufus. "Sit with Pete."

She almost laughed out loud with joy and sank onto the ground beside him. "Can Melissa and Tori sit here too?"

He didn't look up but nodded. "Melissa got M&M's?" He stroked Mouse's fur while he talked.

Melissa giggled as she crossed her legs beneath her on the far side of Rufus and next to where Tori had sat. "Not today, buddy. I'll try to remember to bring some next time, okay?"

He reached for the leash that Colt held and stroked Rufus's fur. "Good boy."

Kate's dad cleared his throat. "Mr. Creighton, Kate tells us you wanted to talk to us. How can we help you? I hope your daughter didn't have a bad experience during the ride or wasn't upset that she didn't win."

The other man shook his head. "Not at all. In fact, other than her horse coming up lame, she seemed to enjoy herself greatly. She was disappointed not to finish the ride, but I told her she's young, and there's always another day." He fisted his hands in his lap. "I'm not sure how to say this, or where to begin."

Kate's mom smiled. "I've found it's best to start at the beginning. Would you care for some iced tea?"

"No, thank you." He drew in a shaky breath, then let it out slowly. "You're right. I'll start at the beginning and get right to the point. I stole your box."

Chapter Twenty

Stunned silence met Mr. Creighton's announcement, and Kate stifled a gasp. He'd stolen their box? But of all the people they'd investigated, he'd been the nicest and the one they least suspected. Besides, he owned a business and didn't seem poor.

Anger blossomed in Kate's heart, and she stared at the man who'd hurt them all. "Why? It didn't belong to you, and it contained the money for the kids who need to attend camp. You must have plenty of money, so why would you do that?" She glanced at her parents, wondering if they'd scold her for talking disrespectfully to an adult, but all they did was nod.

Mr. Creighton turned his face away for a brief moment, his mouth pinched in a tight line. Then he swiveled back to meet Kate's gaze. "I'm afraid I have a problem that I've never admitted or dealt with. I know that doesn't excuse what I did, but it might help to explain. Ever since I've been little, I've been fascinated with antiques—especially ones with rich, beautiful colors. They draw me in, and I almost have an obsession to own them. The day I came to sign my daughter up for the scavenger hunt, I heard an older man grumbling about an antique box your mother owned but wouldn't sell. I didn't think a thing about it until I saw it for myself in the office. Then I had to have it."

Kate's dad frowned. "So you simply took it when you knew how much that money meant to the kids, not to mention how much the box might mean to my wife?"

Mr. Creighton winced but didn't evade the question. "I knew your wife wouldn't sell it, but I had no idea the money was inside. No one touched the box or opened it when I paid. Mrs. Ferris, I assume you must have placed the money in it after I left the office."

She shrugged. "I don't remember, since there were so many people in and out that day, but it's possible. I still don't understand why you took it, or when."

"I knew it was an antique and possibly valuable, but that isn't what drew me. It was the age, the beauty, the workmanship. As to when, I took my daughter home, then returned and waited. I watched the office until I knew no one was inside. I'd brought a large paper bag with me that contained a few grocery items. I slipped into the office, placed the box under a larger item, and then walked out the door to my car." He hung his head. "And I've regretted it ever since."

Colt scowled. "So you're the man who left us the clues, promising we'd find the box? We went to at least two trees with big roots and found nothing. Then we came to your store, and Kate even asked if you knew of any trees that fit that description, but you denied it. Why all the clues with no box, and why lie? That doesn't make a bit of sense."

Mr. Creighton squirmed in his chair, but no one tried to make him feel more comfortable. "Yes, I left the clues. Believe it or not, I did put the box beneath the roots of a large fir tree, but you didn't find the right one. After you came to the store and asked your question, I realized you hadn't found it and probably wouldn't. I knew someone else might find it, so I retrieved it."

Tori bit her lip and glanced at Kate, then back at Mr. Creighton. "But why didn't you just tell us when we were there?"

"Because I was a coward. I didn't want you to know I'd done it. I was hoping you'd find the box from the clues and never figure out it was me."

Kate's dad nodded. "What made you change your mind and come forward now?"

Mr. Creighton hesitated, then looked from Kate to each of her friends. "These kids did. I overheard them talking about it. They have an incredible attitude. They were upset and disappointed, but not vindictive or hateful. It made me ashamed ... more than I've ever been. I've always believed myself to be a good man—a decent person—but now I know I've been lying to myself all along." He sucked in a long, slow breath. "In fact, I find it amazing that not one of you has asked about the box or the money since I told you I took it. Why haven't you demanded it back or called the police? That's what I'd have done if the shoe was on the other foot."

Kate's mom smiled. "I'll admit I'd love to have my great-grandmother's box back, but right now I'm more concerned about you."

The man gave a hard start that jarred the chair. "Me? I don't understand."

She glanced at Kate. "What have we been talking about lately, Kate? Do you want to explain?"

Kate's heart thumped in surprise, but she nodded. "The last couple of weeks, Mom, Dad, Pete, and I have been praying for you. Well, we didn't know it was you, but we've been praying for whoever stole the box. Dad told us the person must be miserable inside to do something like that, and that we needed to pray that God would change him. I told the rest of my friends that we needed to pray, so they have been too. Maybe that's one reason we weren't acting hateful. It's kind of hard to hate someone you're praying for."

Mr. Creighton hung his head and moaned. "I don't know what to say." He lifted his head and stared at everyone. "Would you trust me to go to my car and come right back? I promise I won't try to run."

Kate's dad chuckled. "It wouldn't matter if you did. It's not like we don't know where you live or work. But sure, go ahead." He waved his hand in the direction of the car. "We'll wait."

The man almost bolted from his chair and jogged toward the parking area. He returned in a minute or two, a sack clutched in his hands. He stood next to Kate's mom, then slowly placed the sack in her lap. "I believe this is yours." He continued to stand, as though too afraid of her reaction to sit again.

She gazed at him, then smiled. "Thank you."

His eyes widened. "Aren't you going to open it?"

"I'm sure I know what it contains. But it might be nice for the kids to see that you've returned it." She set the bag on the ground, then opened it.

A soft gasp came from Kate as her mother withdrew the ornate box that had been in their family so many years. "But Mom, how about the money?"

Mr. Creighton stood at attention. "I didn't touch it. The box was locked. As I said earlier, I didn't know it contained the money until I read the article in the paper about the theft." A red wave rose up his neck and into his cheeks. "I had no desire to break the lock on a treasure like this. And the money meant nothing to me. However, that's when I realized what I'd done and how terribly selfish—and wrong—my actions had been. I'd destroyed the joy of children who hoped to attend camp, as well as hurt you children's faith in others. I'm so sorry."

Kate looked at her parents. "What now?"

Mr. Creighton raised a hand. "Please. There's one other thing." He reached into his back pocket and pulled out a wallet. He flipped it open, withdrew a check, and handed it to Kate's dad. "I know this won't make up for what I did, or change the fact that I'm a thief—and I don't expect it to. But all the same, I'd like you to have this."

Kate's father glanced down, then up at Mr. Creighton and frowned. "Why would you give me a check for a thousand dollars?"

Mr. Creighton turned red again. "It's not a bribe. You do what you think is right concerning the theft. That's up to you. As far as the check, I was hoping you might use it with the rest of the money, to allow more children to attend camp. That's all."

Kate's dad gave a slow nod. "I see." He looked at Kate's mom. "Nan? Your thoughts?"

She didn't hesitate. "Mr. Creighton, do you and your daughter attend church anywhere?"

He appeared taken aback. "Uh … no. We haven't attended since my wife died seven years ago." He dipped his head. "I guess I blamed God for her death … and I've been angry ever since."

Just like Melissa was when her dad left and things started falling apart, Kate thought. *Before she met us and began to realize that God really does care.* Kate sighed. *And like I am sometimes when things don't go the way I expect them to. Then I blame God or doubt Him.*

Kate's mom tipped her head toward Mr. Creighton. "How would you and your daughter like to attend with us tomorrow, then come here for dinner afterward?"

Kate gulped. This wasn't at all what she'd expected. "Mom? Dad? You aren't going to call the police and turn Mr. Creighton in?" She wanted to shout, *After everything he put us all through?* But she didn't.

Melissa stared at Kate's mom. "Yeah. That's what I figured you'd do, first thing. I couldn't believe you didn't have him hauled off as soon as he admitted he stole the box. What's the deal, anyway?"

Kate's mom smiled. "I guess you haven't been around us long enough yet, Melissa, to know we do things a little differently. We're told in the Bible to forgive our enemies and to pray for people who treat us badly." She directed her attention to Mr. Creighton. "You did treat us badly when you stole the box, and we've been praying for you. But God caused you to think about what you'd done, and you returned our property. Not only that, you've shown remorse, admitted you were wrong, and said you have a problem."

Kate's dad raised his brows. "I think at this point"—he glanced at Kate's mom, who nodded—"we need to forgive and try to help you deal with your issues, rather than punish you when you've finally come to the place where you know you need help."

At that moment silence descended on the group, and something nudged Kate's heart. She and her friends hadn't been totally honest with Jerry and invaded his private space without his permission—he had the right to be upset and suspicious. Even if he wasn't nice to Jake, they might need to apologize. And worse than that, they'd treated Mr. Wallace badly, a lonely old man who mostly had magazines and newspapers for company. Sure, they'd brought him cookies, but they'd done it so they could snoop through his house. They'd also made a mess of his treasures. The old man was confused and had issues, but they hadn't helped him. Instead, they'd done what Melissa said they shouldn't do with Jake—they'd used him to get what they wanted.

Kate felt even more terrible now for leaving Mr. Wallace so upset. She decided that as soon as her parents rested up a bit from the scavenger hunt, she would talk to her mom again about him. It wasn't enough to invite the elderly man over for dinner or to church. Maybe together the five friends could figure out other ways to help, like cleaning his kitchen, asking him about his collections, or doing little things the way they did for Mrs. Maynard. Maybe he was cranky because he needed a friend.

Just like she had needed friends when she moved to Odell ... and found Tori, Colt, Melissa, and now, Jake.

"Right." Kate gave a decisive nod to her dad's statement. "I agree. We got the money back ... and a lot more too. Dad, you said we needed a miracle to be able to pay for Pete's camp. Now we can send Pete—and a bunch of other kids!" Then she sobered. "What's more important, though, is that Mr. Creighton won't steal anymore, and we know God can help him with that."

A tear trickled down Mr. Creighton's cheek. He didn't even try to wipe it away.

"Mr. Creighton, we'll keep praying for you," Kate said softly, "but let us know if we can do other things to help too. That's what friends do. Right, guys?" She looked at each of her friends.

A ringing chorus of joy sounded from the group. Pete clapped, Mouse and Rufus barked, and a horse in the nearby pasture neighed.

Mr. Creighton buried his face in his hands. "Thank you all. I didn't know people like you existed."

Jake snorted. "Hey, this is just like that movie—"

"Jake!" Kate and her other friends all said at once. "Give it a rest," Kate added, "and we promise you can keep hanging out with us."

He grinned at the circle of new friends. "Cool. That's even better than watching *Star Wars*!"

When a rockin' concert comes to an end,
the audience might cheer for an encore.
When a tasty meal comes to an end,
it's always nice to savor a bit of dessert.
When a great story comes to an end,
we think you may want to linger.
And so we offer …

… just a little something more after
you have finished a David C Cook novel.
We invite you to stay awhile in the story.

Thanks for reading!

Turn the page for …

Secrets for Your Diary

Secret #1

Do you believe that dreams can come true?

It isn't in the budget for Pete to go to camp. Kate's dad says it will take a miracle. Kate can't accept that the dream isn't within reach. Instead, she determines to find a way to make it happen and asks her friends to brainstorm with her.

Is there something you dream of doing? Or that you could do to help a person in need? What could you do to put a plan in motion?

Note from Kate

At first I was super-disappointed that Pete couldn't go to camp and scared that Dad might decide to close the barn. Then I realized Pete was more important than the barn, and God might show us a way to keep the barn open and to help Pete. My friends and I brainstormed to come up with a fun idea, and the scavenger hunt even brought new people to our barn who might decide to board there. If you've got a problem or you know someone else who does, maybe, with God's help and the help of your friends, you can brainstorm a new way to tackle it!

Secret #2

Is it easy for you to add friends to your group?

Kate and her friends finally get used to Melissa being a part of their group. Then Colt suggests they get to know Jake. But Kate worries about what Jake might be like, especially because his brother had been mean to him all his life. Still, she can't shake what Melissa says about not using Jake—that they shouldn't get something from him and then dump him.

What about you? Do you make friends just for what you can get from them (like status in a group), or because you find them interesting and want to get to know them?

Note from Kate

When I first met Jake, I thought he was kind of annoying—until I got to know him better. Now I realize he has a funny sense of humor and is different, but different isn't always bad. In fact, since he's been hanging around, I think I'd miss his silly movie references and big words if I never saw him again. That makes me sad that I didn't want him to be part of our group at first. I didn't want to include anyone else, because what we had seemed perfect. I'm so glad I was willing to give him a chance. How about you? Is there someone who doesn't have many friends that you can be kind to?

Secret #3

Do you ever feel impatient with people who say or do things that aren't kind? Or people who always seem to be angry about life?

Kate learns a lot about judging others. She realizes that you can't possibly know what makes people act the way they do if you don't know anything about their past or their life at home.

For example, Melissa used to be mean to Kate and Tori. But Melissa's dad had left her and her mom almost broke, and that had sent Melissa's mom into a spiral of drinking. Melissa was sad and lonely, and her friends turned away from her when they discovered she was no longer wealthy.

Mr. Creighton lost his wife seven years earlier and blamed God. His anger against God made him bitter and the kind of man who would steal.

How can this perspective—that life situations can cause people to act as they do— change the way you think of others and how patient you are with them?

Note from Kate

This was a superhard thing for me to deal with at first, because I thought Melissa was a stuck-up girl who didn't care about anyone but herself. Wow! Was I ever wrong! I didn't realize how much pain she was stuffing inside because of things going on in her family. The same with Mr. Creighton. I wanted to be mad at him because he stole Mom's box and our money, until I heard his story. Now if someone doesn't treat me right, I pray for that person, try being nice, and wait to see what happens. You might want to try the same thing too. Maybe you'll find out that person has a horrible family life and is very unhappy inside. You might be the one God uses to make a difference in that person's life and attitude. Now wouldn't that be cool?

A Horse-Themed Scavenger Hunt

You can plan your own horse-themed scavenger hunt with friends, and you don't even have to own a horse! (Of course, if you own a horse, that's fine too. Just set up the hunt for horseback.) It doesn't matter where you live—in town with a small yard, in a city apartment with no yard, or on a farm with lots of land. These ideas work anywhere.

Setting Up the Scavenger Hunt

1. Make a list of horse-related items you can use for your scavenger hunt. Some you might already have, and others are inexpensive to buy. Here are a few ideas to get you started:

  * a hairbrush (instead of a horse brush)
  * twine (instead of a lead rope)
  * an apple
  * sugar cubes (horses love to eat them)
  I'm sure you'll think of lots more!

2. Brainstorm horse-related clues for each item that give hints of what scavenger hunters should look for. Decide whether you're going to have individual scavenger hunters or hunters working together in groups. Make enough copies of the clues so that each person or group has their own list. Examples of items to find and clues:

* Item to find: a hairbrush
Clue: Without this, you and your horse would have wild hair and a tangled mane.
* Item to find: twine
Clue: It's hard to lead a horse anywhere without this.
* Item to find: an apple
Clue: This not only keeps the doctor away, but horses love them!
* Item to find: sugar cubes
Clue: There's nothing more sweet, and it makes a horse smack his lips to get one.

3. Hide the items where they can be found, but not in obvious places. For example, don't put the hairbrushes in the bathroom or bedroom. Place them in the kitchen or TV room, but don't hide them so well that searchers make a mess hunting for them. The adults in your home might not appreciate that!

4. Come up with a few creative prizes. You can use fun items you already have or inexpensive items you buy. You can give one prize to each person who completes the list, rather than only having one winner. That makes the scavenger hunt fun for everyone. Depending on the age of your hunters, prizes could be packs of stickers, gum or pieces of candy, a book, or a blank journal. Use your imagination!

When You're Ready to Launch Your Scavenger Hunt

1. Give each scavenger hunter or group the list of clues.

2. Set a time limit. Everyone has to bring their items back within thirty minutes, an hour, or whatever time you choose.

3. Give out the prizes at the end. And most of all, have fun!

Author's Note

I've been an avid horse lover all of my life. I can't remember a time when I wasn't fascinated with the idea of owning a horse, although it didn't happen until after I married. My family lived in a small town on a couple of acres that were mostly steep hillside, so other than our lawn and garden area, there was no room for a horse. I lived out my dreams by reading every book I could find that had anything to do with horses.

My first horse was a two-year-old Arabian gelding named Nicky, who taught me so much and caused me to fall deeply in love with the Arabian breed. Over the years we've owned a stallion, a number of mares, a handful of foals, and a couple of geldings. It didn't take too many years to discover I couldn't make money in breeding. After losing a mare and baby due to a reaction to penicillin, and having another mare reject her baby at birth, we decided it was time to leave that part of the horse industry and simply enjoy owning a riding horse or two.

Our daughter, Marnee, brought loving horses to a whole new level. She was begging to ride when she was two to three years old and was riding her own pony alone at age five. Within a few years, she requested lessons, as she wanted to switch from

Western trail riding to showing English, both in flat work and hunt-seat, and later, in basic dressage. I learned so much listening to her instructor and watching that I decided to take lessons myself.

We spent a couple of years in the show world, but Marnee soon discovered she wanted to learn for the sake of improving her own skills more than competing, and she became a first-rate horsewoman.

We still ride together, as she and her husband, Brian, own property next to ours. My old Arabian mare, Khaila, was my faithful trail horse for over seventeen years and lived with Marnee's horses on their property, so she wouldn't be lonely. At the age of twenty-six, she began having serious age-related problems and went on to horse heaven in late July of 2013. Now I ride Brian's Arabian mare, Sagar, when Marnee and I trail-ride. I am so blessed to have a daughter who shares the same love as me and to have had so many wonderful years exploring the countryside with my faithful horse Khaila.

If you don't own your own horse yet, don't give up. It might not happen while you still live at home, and you might have to live out your dreams in books, or even by taking a lesson at a local barn, but that's okay. God knows your desire and will help fulfill it in His perfect way.

Acknowledgments

This series has been a brand-new adventure for me—one I never expected, but one I'm so blessed to have experienced. I've loved horses all my life and owned them since I was nineteen, but I never thought I'd write horse novels for girls. I'm so glad I was wrong!

So many people have helped make this series possible: My friends at church, who were excited when I shared God's prompting and offered to pray that the project would find a home, as well as my family, my friends, and my critique group, who believed in me, listened, read my work, and cheered me on. There have also been a number of authors who helped me brainstorm ideas for the series or specific sections of one book or the other when I struggled—Kimberly, Vickie, Margaret, Cheryl, Lissa, Nancy—you've all been such a blessing!

My fan group and Street Team on Facebook helped me brainstorm ideas for the sleuthing the kids could do to try to find the thief, and my editor's daughter, Kayla, gave me ideas for the scavenger hunt. Books are rarely written completely alone, and I'm so thankful for the help of friends and readers.

I also want to thank the team at David C Cook. I was so thrilled when Don Pape asked if I'd consider sending this series to him to review when I mentioned I was writing it. The horse lovers on the committee snatched it up and galloped with it, and I was so excited! I love working with this company and pray we'll have many more years and books together. Thank you to all who made this a possibility and, we pray, a resounding success!

You can learn more about me and all of my books at www.miraleeferrell.com. Thank you for taking the time to read this series!

About the Author

Miralee Ferrell, the author of the Horses and Friends series plus twelve other novels, was always an avid reader. She started collecting first-edition Zane Grey Westerns as a young teen. But she never felt the desire to write books … until after she turned fifty. Inspired by Zane Grey and old Western movies, she decided to write stories set in the Old West in the 1880s.

After she wrote her first Western novel, *Love Finds You in Last Chance, California*, she was hooked. Her *Love Finds You in Sundance, Wyoming* won the Will Rogers Medallion Award for Western fiction, and Universal Studios requested a copy of her debut novel, *The Other Daughter*, for a potential family movie.

Miralee loves horseback riding on the wooded trails near her home with her married daughter, who lives nearby, and spending time with her granddaughter, Kate. Besides her horse friends, she's owned cats, dogs (a six-pound, long-haired Chihuahua named Lacey was often curled up on her lap as she wrote this book), rabbits, chickens, and even two cougars,

Spunky and Sierra, rescued from breeders who couldn't care for them properly.

Miralee would love to hear from you:

www.miraleeferrell.com (blog, newsletter, and website)
www.twitter.com/miraleeferrell
www.facebook.com/miraleeferrell
www.facebook.com/groups/82316202888 (fan group)

Books by Miralee Ferrell

Horses and Friends Series
A Horse for Kate
Silver Spurs
Mystery Rider
Blue Ribbon Trail Ride

Love Blossoms in Oregon Series
Blowing on Dandelions
Forget Me Not
Wishing on Buttercups
Dreaming on Daisies

The 12 Brides of Christmas Series
The Nativity Bride

The 12 Brides of Summer Series
The Dogwood Blossom Bride

Love Finds You Series
Love Finds You in Bridal Veil, Oregon
Recently republished as *Finding Love in Bridal Veil, Oregon*
Love Finds You in Sundance, Wyoming
Love Finds You in Last Chance, California
Love Finds You in Tombstone, Arizona
(sequel to *Love Finds You in Last Chance, California*)
Recently republished as *Finding Love in Tombstone, Arizona*
The Other Daughter
Finding Jeena (sequel to *The Other Daughter*)

Other Contributions/Compilations
A Cup of Comfort for Cat Lovers
Fighting Fear: Winning the War at Home
Faith & Finances: In God We Trust
Faith & Family: A Christian Living Daily
Devotional for Parents and Their Kids